SOMETHING FAR AWAY AND HAPPY

BRYCE OAKLEY

ALSO BY BRYCE OAKLEY

The Adventurers

Something Far Away and Happy

Against The Grain

Never Mine

Every Version

Latitude & Longing

One Last Run

Shift the Tide

Holiday Romances

Most Wonderful

All Aglow

Ghosted Christmas Past

The Snowy Springs Holiday Romances

Baking Spirits Bright

Rebel Without A Claus

The Kaleidoscope Album

Undone

Bewilder

Midnight

Bloom

Revel

The Kaleidoscope Album Box Set

CONTENTS

PROLOGUE

SEPTEMBER 2009

JULIA

"YOU WANT TO GET OUT OF HERE?" SHE ASKED, LEANING IN
so I could hear her over the suffocatingly loud bass beat,
letting me feel her warm breath against my neck.

Fuck. Yes.

Remington Van der Meer was asking me to "get out of"
somewhere, and also hopefully to "get out of" my clothes.

We'd only officially met a few days before in our
poetry workshop, an elective I had chosen because I
thought it'd be easy, but was quick to realize I was wrong.
In a small college like McManus, I'd known about Remi
for years. We didn't run in the same circles—she hung out
with the sporty lesbians and I was committed to the nerdy
pre-med crowd. Still, I knew her love 'em and leave 'em
reputation, but I'd just broken up with Curtis and thought
maybe a fun night would be good for me.

"Maybe," I shrugged, leaning on the wall as I swirled
my drink around in my cup. The party had expanded past
the reaches of the dorm hours ago, and we were standing

11

in a crowded hallway, next to a girl pulling a plastic bag of wine out of her purse.

Seduction Central, it was not.

"My roommate is studying back at mine. What about yours?" Her cocky swagger complemented her oh-I-casu-ally-threw-this-on-even-though-I-look-incredible outfit—ripped black jeans, a loose short-sleeved button-down with the neck so far unbuttoned that I fully expected to see her breasts at any moment.

I mean, one could hope.

"Oh, you think it's like that?" I teased, lifting a brow.

Was it possible for my pounding heart to bust through my ribcage? How was I even expected to speak at a time like this, when I wanted to squeal instead? Why did she have me in her sights, of all people?

She placed a hand on the wall near my head, leaning in again. God, she was so close, I could practically feel her mouth on my lips. "Isn't it?"

I grinned, my cheeks flushing as I raised my eyes to meet hers.

"I know a place. If you don't mind a little breaking and entering." She winked, straightening her posture and holding out her hand. "Trust me?"

"Not one bit." I placed my hand in hers.

"Shh," Remi whispered a little too loudly, and I held my hand over my mouth to hide an excited laugh, watching as she stood on her tiptoes to push open the high window of the darkened building.

"That's way too high. There's no way I'm getting through that," I tried to whisper.

She stepped back, kneeling and patting her knee as though it was a platform. "A boost, m'lady."

"Okay, but when I break my arm from this, I want it on the record it was your fault." I couldn't help but laugh as I tried to look accusingly at her.

"I take full responsibility for what a good idea this is." She smiled up at me with excitement.

I climbed up, and as I struggled to fit my shoulders through the window, she gave my ass a playful slap—a cheeky move for a woman who hadn't even kissed me yet —as I wiggled my hips past the frame, falling into a heap on the other side.

Thank god she hadn't seen that.

I stood quickly, fixing my hair as I watched her climb through the window behind me, her Bieber-length blonde hair flopping in front of her eyes as she grinned mischievously, a perfect dimple popping on her cheek.

She landed beside me, still grinning in that wolfish way that made me weak in the knees…among other places.

She was nearly six feet of broad, muscled strength, complete with thick, wavy hair and twinkling blue eyes. She was drop-dead gorgeous—hands down and popularly known as the hottest woman at McManus, our small liberal, private college, though I doubt she'd have trouble maintaining that honor anywhere.

I had always thought she was a bit of an egotistical asshole, the kind who knew exactly just how fucking gorgeous she was.

I half-expected to be a one-night stand for Ms. Remington Van der Meer, or even for her to be a one-night stand for me.

The air between us heated as I stared up at her.

She ran a hand through her hair, biting her lip.

I couldn't help myself. I threw myself at her, wrapping my arms around her neck, pulling her to kiss me. If she was surprised, she didn't show it. Her mouth was warm and demanding, her tongue and hands claiming me as her fingers trailed their way down my back. Her tongue tasted like tequila and lime, her lips the salt.

She broke our kiss and took my hand, looking up and down the hallway.

"This way," she whispered, and led me down the hall to the student lounge.

Though it wasn't big by any means, there were couches and chairs, and most importantly, no one else around.

She led me to a couch, pulling me into her lap as she pulled my mouth back to hers. I straddled her, trying to bite back a groan as her hips moved under my own. Wow, who knew how quickly things could move once we had a taste of one another?

She was already shameless. Her hands explored my body, rising and falling over my curves as she continued to kiss me, her mouth soft and commanding all at once. I loved it.

"Julia, I've wanted you so fucking bad," she growled into my neck.

"You have?" I teased, twisting on her lap, holding my mane of curls away from my face. She probably said that to every girl she slept with, but that simple sentence made me feel so sexy, so desired, especially in a position where my body was on full display—something that typically made me feel panicked, not empowered.

I couldn't understand why she was looking at *me* like that. Me: nerdy with glasses, big curls, wide hips...She could have anyone, and she was here with me.

Remi gripped my hips, pulling me into hers. "For so long."

My stomach flipped. She was good at this.

"And I think you want me, too," she said, her voice low.

"Yes," I moaned, moving my hands to her chest as I closed my eyes, but she stilled. When I opened my eyes again, afraid I'd touched her when I shouldn't have, she looked up at me as though I was pure magic, like she was in awe. She weaved a hand into my curls and tightened her fist, not pulling, but holding me. She gently tugged my face to press her forehead to mine.

"Are you sure?" She asked in a small voice.

I gazed into her eyes in surprise and confusion. I'd never imagined her to be vulnerable. I didn't think she had a vulnerable bone in her body. Or a patient one, even.

"Wh-what?"

"Are you sure you want this?" Her eyes searched mine. "Have you ever…"

"I'm not the Virgin Mary, if that's what you're asking," I teased, trying to lighten the suddenly very heavy mood.

I'd never been with a woman, but that didn't mean I would be entirely in the dark about what to do—I had certainly been finding out what my own body responded to, as well as my fair share of, uh, pop culture research.

"I don't want you to regret anything," she said.

I definitely hadn't been expecting that. I paused, studying her. It was as if she was an entirely different person at the moment, not a hint of the arrogance that I simultaneously hated and was drawn to. Was she nervous? I never thought I'd see the moment that *the* Remi Van der Meer needed reassurance.

"Let me show you," I said, feeling emboldened in the moment. I took her hand, guiding it down the front of my jeans so that she could feel exactly how ready I was, how much I wanted her.

Her eyes widened in surprise and she shifted, angling her shoulder to leverage her arm in an otherwise awkward position as her fingers explored further.

"Do you believe me now?" I smirked, my stomach twisting as she continued to touch me.

She grinned, and I could almost see her confidence and playfulness return, every stroke of her fingertips building us both up.

She flipped me so that I was on my back on the couch, and she lay beside me, kissing and nipping at my lips and neck as her hand made short work of fully unbuttoning my pants and returning to touch me.

I was surprised by how gentle and focused she was, even though I could tell she was eager. I had always slept with guys who thought foreplay was a means to an end, some afterthought, or worse, a favor.

Her fingers circled my clit in easy, languorous swipes as my body responded accordingly, my back arching, my hips pressing into her hand, a kind of pleasure rising in my body that I'd never felt before.

I closed my eyes and heard myself moan loudly and felt horrifically embarrassed until I looked up to see Remi beaming down at me.

"Sorry, I—"

"It's like you've never been touched," she said in a tone that reminded me of whispered wonder.

"Not like this." I felt my cheeks heat with the confession.

Remi's expression darkened as she dipped her head low, taking my mouth in hers as she increased the pressure of her fingers.

"Just slightly lower," I instructed.

She moved her hand, groaning as if my direction had turned her on, not offended her.

The heady combination of this gorgeous woman showering me with attention and the idea that we could get caught at any time was almost too much. I took a long, deep breath in to calm down.

She lowered her hand, pushing a finger inside of me as her thumb continued circling my clit.

"Oh fuck," I said, the pressure building inside of me. Okay, forget calming down. "More."

"You are so fucking sexy," she whispered in my ear, taking the lobe between her teeth. She slowly pushed another finger into me while holding my stare.

I never thought eye contact would be so incredibly intimate.

As she hit the exact spot I needed her most, I was thrown over the edge, my mind consumed in a flurry of bright yellows and reds, my cries buried in her kiss as her hips held me steady, her fingers continuing whatever magic they had begun.

I grabbed her wrist, pulling her hand away as I grew too sensitive. My chest heaved as I tried to catch my breath.

"You look like a world, waiting to surrender," she said, kissing down my cheek and nipping at my neck.

Wait, I recognized that line.

"Did you just pull out Neruda to woo me? Because I think we're past the wooing."

"Not even close."

I stared up at her, surprised again and again. I had no idea what I was getting myself into, and yet, my heart was already softening.

I swallowed. "I think it's my turn."

She blinked.

"What, you thought I was a Pillow Princess?"

"Wow, pulling out the lingo." She smirked.

"I've seen *The L Word*, I know what's up," I joked.

In truth, I had secretly watched every episode of *The L*

Word that summer after my parents had gone to bed, holding the remote and ready to change the channel at the slightest hint that they might wake up and walk into the living room where our only TV was.

"Then, you're an expert, no doubt." She laughed, her mouth wide in amusement, her head tipping back to elongate her neck before me.

I leaned forward, kissing the soft, smooth skin of her throat.

"Now lean back, because I'm about to go full Shane on this situation," I said.

She laughed again, shaking her head. "Oh no, please, never say anything like that ever again," she said with an easy grin.

"Jeez, okay, not a Shane kind of girl, I see." I tried to look as judgmental as possible.

She laughed again, giving me a quick kiss that felt instantly so familiar. "You are so weird. I had no idea. I thought I was just asking out a very normal, cute girl in my class, not Alice Pieszecki."

"Well, sorry to disappoint, not normal at all," I teased, buttoning my jeans as I pushed up onto my knees.

"Just cute," Remi said, resting a hand beneath her head as she gazed up at me with a smile that only quirked one edge of her mouth.

Why did that look make the breath catch in my throat? I had always thought she was attractive, but truly, she was stunning, especially with flushed cheeks and those sparkling blue eyes.

"Okay, real question, though. I've always wanted to try, um…" I gestured to the area in question. "Doing that." I nodded to punctuate the thought, wetting my lips, my mouth feeling dry with nerves.

She gave me a bemused smirk. "Oh, have you just?"

I nodded, taking a deep breath. "I may need some input from you, though."

"Well, as much as I applaud your bravery and your…" She paused as though looking for the right word. "Gumption, why don't I show you exactly what I like first?"

"How do you plan on doing that?" I asked, glancing from her hips to her face.

She hooked an arm around my waist, pulling me back down on top of her. "Oh, I have a few ideas."

Who knows how long we stayed on that gross, scratchy couch, too enveloped in our own world to care that we were in the student union—hours? Lifetimes? I felt worshipped in a way I never had before, and I felt brave and confident enough to try things, to learn and adjust and do literally anything to hear her moan my name.

Her taste, the way she bit her lip as my tongue explored her.

I knew even then that I was a goner. I was hers, whether I knew what that meant or not.

WE HAD BEEN DATING for six months, but it was as if we'd always been together. When I wasn't in class or pre-med club meetings, I was with her. We'd even enrolled in an advanced poetry workshop again.

The perk of a small school like ours was that even though we were both seniors, almost everyone still lived on campus. The downside to living on campus was that we had to be creative with privacy. We both had fairly understanding roommates, but there was usually a massive party on her floor, and, well, I lived on a quiet floor and Remi had discovered many things that made me anything but quiet.

We spent the fall and winter desperate for one another.

In shower stalls, in private library study rooms, anywhere we could find in the towering mountains surrounding campus.

It was as though we couldn't get enough of each other. I felt insatiable, chaotic. More alive than I had ever been before.

At the moment, we had just fogged up the windows of the car. We'd parked on some back mountain road, folding down the backseats of my small SUV to have some semblance of space.

Remi was between my legs, wiping at her mouth as I caught my breath, coming back down to earth.

"I love you," I whispered, breathless, my heart pounding in my chest. "So much."

Her brow furrowed as she bent forward, moving as she held my naked body tightly to her own. "I love you, too," she said, barely loud enough for me to hear.

I softened into her, nuzzling my head into the crook of her neck.

"*I have gone marking the atlas of your body with crosses of fire.*" She trailed a finger up my bare arm.

I smiled, tears stinging at the corners of my eyes, overflowing, endless happiness in the moment. Six months ago, I'd have never guessed Remi would be reciting my favorite poem to me. Now, I knew what a hopeless romantic she was. She'd memorized it the day I told her I liked it.

Surprised again and again.

"Tell me something far away and happy, then," I said, quoting another line from the poem.

"I want you to come with me."

I laughed. "I think I already have, baby, but if you—"

"No, I mean, come with me next year." She didn't have to explain more for me to know what she meant. Earlier

that week, we found out she had been accepted to MIT's
MBA program and would be moving to Boston in the fall.
The realization that our time together had an expiration
date had made everything feel a bit more frantic. It was
only March, but Spring Break was in a week, and after, in a
month and a half, we'd graduate.

I swallowed, my throat tightening with emotion. "You
don't—"

She put her hands on my shoulders, moving me to look
her in the eye. "I mean it, Jude. It's you and me. I want to
be with you and in a few years, we can get married and
have tons of dogs."

I studied her, feeling suddenly wary. I knew that the
last six months had been the best of my life, and that I
loved her with a ferocity that I had never felt before, but
we were 22. Was she really ready to settle down? Was I?

"And tons of babies," she added.

I laughed, surprised by the statement. Remi had never
mentioned kids before, and although I really wanted
them in the future, that was so far ahead of where we
were.

"But what will I do? You know, for med school? I
haven't even gotten my scores back yet." I wanted to
laugh hysterically, simultaneously feeling like it was a
crazy idea and at the same time, feeling joyful and excited,
like it could happen.

She paused, biting at my lower lip. "I think they have
med schools in Boston, babe. It's not like time or money is
an issue. I'll get my inheritance as soon as I graduate from
here. And I'll support you, no matter what, you know
that." She looked up at me through her thick lashes and
my stomach swirled and leaped. I wanted to agree so
badly.

"You haven't thought this through, Rem," I said,

smiling and tilting my head sideways. "I'm flattered, but—"

"I know what I want," she interrupted, fisting my hair and kissing me roughly again. She sounded breathless when she pulled away. "I love you. I am in love with you. And I always will be. I promise."

I put my hands over my eyes, steadying myself and trying to clear my thoughts. It was so hard to think properly when she was near, when she was kissing me and touching me, and our naked bodies were entwined.

"How can you promise that?" I asked.

"When my mind's made up, there's no stopping me," she grinned.

Well, *that* I knew to be true.

She looked down at me, raking her fingernails gently down my back, leaving goosebumps in their wake. "You love me, too. Tell me you've ever felt this way about someone before."

I paused, shaking my head.

"You're *it* for me," she said, her voice tender.

I believed her. I did. My throat tightened and I quickly blinked back tears. I threw my arms around her neck, burying my face in her shoulder to avoid letting her see me cry.

"Anything is possible as long as we're together," Remi said. "I'll always take care of you. Don't cry, baby."

I wanted nothing more than to say yes.

So I did.

ON THE FIRST day of Spring Break, I was sitting in my room planning what I'd take with me to Boston. I'd already told my parents—they'd met Remi over Christmas break when

she'd visited and they were just as enamored with her as
I was.

My laptop dinged a notification for a new email. Curious, I stood up, crossed the room, and opened it.

No subject. Remington Van der Meer was the supposed sender, except it wasn't her usual email address I recognized.

There was no text, only a link to a New York Times article. My heart started pounding, seeing the URL. Engagement. Van der Meer. Dawes.

"Miss Remington Van der Meer and Miss Alison Dawes are happy to announce their engagement. The two met in third grade and the rest is history." The article continued on, but all I could see was a photo of the two of them, smiling.

It was recent. I could tell because I had given Remi that sweater for Christmas.

She was supposed to be back in Virginia for Spring Break telling her parents about me joining her in Boston.

Was this a joke? Was this a very, very bad prank?

Or, had they been together while she had been at school, promising me all of those wonderful things about a life together?

No, it had to be a joke. I believed her when she told me she'd never felt this way before. She promised to always love me. It couldn't be real.

I picked up my phone to call Remi.

She picked up on the third ring. "Never call me again," she bit out, her voice making my blood feel ice cold in my veins.

"Rem—"

"Never. I *never* want to talk to you again," she said.

I barely recognized her voice.

I hung up the phone without saying anything more. My entire body began to shake.

So then, was it true? How long had Remi and this Alison girl been together?

My knees gave out under me, and suddenly I was on the ground with no recollection of falling.

I called her again, but it rang once and went to voicemail. I called again. And again. Hundreds of times.

I gave her hundreds of chances to take it back. To assure me it wasn't true.

But something was horribly wrong. She never wanted to speak to *me* again, after I learned of her engagement in the goddamn New York Times.

The sinking realization began to set in that it was all a lie, and I was the fool who had agreed to it.

It hurt so bad I couldn't breathe. It hurt so deeply, so shockingly, that I thought for a second my heart would stop. I began to sob, wrapping my arms around my knees, curling into a ball.

I reached for my computer, pulling up her Facebook profile, but she had already blocked me.

I sent a quick email asking her to call me in one last-ditch effort, but it returned immediately, saying it couldn't be sent.

Denial turned to despair began to turn to rage within me. Remington Van der Meer was a liar, and I had believed everything she had told me. I had fallen for it like an idiot. She had used me. She had given me false promises. And for what? To what end?

I was never going to make the mistake of trusting her again. She would *never* get a second chance.

CHAPTER ONE

AUGUST 2020

JULIA

I WASN'T SURE MY WINDSHIELD WIPERS WERE GOING TO survive. They were moving so fast that I imagined them flying off of my car at any moment, but I was still having trouble seeing the road immediately in front of me.

"Turn left," my phone instructed, and I pulled onto a dirt road in the middle of nowhere. It was pouring, but I could see that the road had a sudden bazillion foot drop on the one side, and of course, it had no guard rails.

Well, it was not entirely in the middle of nowhere, but definitely close. I had been driving out of town for the past twenty minutes, I hadn't seen another car for the past ten minutes, and according to my navigation, I was still ten minutes away. This client was a real hermit.

To be honest, I knew nothing about her. Her personal assistant, a woman named Kelly, had called me last week, requesting my interior design services for a large mountain cabin.

"She needs a big change," Kelly had said. "She just finalized a divorce and can't have anything remind her of the ex, if you know what I mean."

Personally, I'd have been pissed if my assistant had told someone else that much about my personal life, but I was secretly pretty grateful for the heads up.

The project was going to be a pretty simple cash cow of a decorating gig, and I sure as hell wasn't in a position to back away from a job just because the client was having a difficult time. Divorce seemed way too messy – I thanked my lucky stars that I had never been married. Marriage and relationships just weren't in the cards for me. Once, I had come close to having a woman propose – my college sweetheart, in fact, but it had turned out to be all wrong – wrong timing, wrong girl.

But I was lucky, in a way. Because that girl had broken my heart, I had dropped out of college and my pre-med classes. I got internships and pursued what I really wanted, and then worked my ass off as I climbed my way up in the interior design world. Not far enough, considering I'd just been turned down for two big boutique hotel projects that I desperately wanted after being told that I didn't have enough big projects in my portfolio. Seriously, what was that about — *we love what you do, but you don't have enough experience, so we're not going to give you that experience?*

My clients loved my work, even if it was mainly just kitchen and bedroom re-dos. I was nowhere near having my own line at Pottery Barn, but that wasn't really my style anyway. I was a vintage lover, personally. My real selling point was finding unique, one-of-a-kind pieces for my clients by scouring antique stores and estate sales, then refinishing them to fit my client's style.

That, and I had a good eye for the small details.

Anyone could slap gray paint and quartz in a room and call it a day. I was determined to make every room tailored more to the client than my own taste.

My personal style leaned much closer to Jonathan Adler than Joana Gaines, but when it came to clients, I was flexible on the subject of farmhouse decor and even shiplap.

My phone rang and I startled, surprised I even got service. I glanced at the dash to see my best friend's name pop up as I clicked the button on the steering wheel to answer it over my car speakers.

"Do you think cars float?" I yelled over the rain as I answered.

"I think it's safe to say that cars do whatever is the opposite of floating," Cameron said.

What a mood killer.

"I just wanted to check on you, because your location says 'Middle of Nowhere' and I know you had that job up in Breck today," Cam continued. "So, want to drop a pin when you get there so I know where to send Search and Rescue?"

"Very thoughtful." I rolled my eyes, slowing down to take a turn.

"Maybe she'll be cute."

"What?"

"The client. A divorcee. Rich. Mountain home. Might be a fun one." Cameron laughed like an evil genius, really leaning into the Mwua-ha-has of it.

"I do *not* sleep with clients," I scoffed. Granted, I'd never had a client I wanted to sleep with before.

I could just picture Cameron's nose crinkling with a knowing grin. "You don't sleep with anybody."

"Hey now." Thankfully, with work, I was too busy to focus on love. Or even lust. I hadn't had a girlfriend in…

well, the fact that I had to pause and think was sad in its own right. Truthfully, other things in my life were so much more important and more fulfilling. My career was taking off, I was working all the time, and I had plenty of vibrators for the nights I felt a little lonely.

"I love you, my little celibate pal," Cameron said.

"Well, not all of us can be Tik Tok lesbians drowning in hot babes."

"Drowning is a strong word. We could say over-flowing."

"Your cup overfloweth," I said with a laugh.

"But I'm serious about the p—"

The phone cracked and cut out. I glanced at the screen to see the call dropped.

I must have lost service.

The car jostled as I hit dips and bumps in the dirt road. Great, the rain was already washing the lane out from under me. I wondered if I would even make it to the place, much less be able to make it back out. I envisioned having to stay in a house with some angsty divorced lady. I shuddered. No, thanks. I did *not* like Chardonnay enough to endure that mashup.

My little, old, late 90s hatchback was still great in the snow, but I had doubts about its abilities to trek out of a sinkhole.

I contemplated turning around.

No, I needed this money and this project for my portfolio.

I drove through an archway that read *Peak 8 Ranch*, over a small bridge that crossed what should have been a creek, but now seemed more like a rushing river almost bursting at the banks. The house was up a small drive from the bridge.

I pulled up to the address from my navigation and

looked out the windshield. Kelly had sent pictures, but I just assumed the angle made it look larger than it was. In truth, this wasn't a cabin. It was some kind of woodsy mansion that happened to be on a mountain. There was nothing cozy or rustic about the exterior, minus the vaguely A-frame shape of the three-story windows lining the front of the place.

I put the car in park and glanced in my visor mirror. I had spent an hour straightening my hair that morning, but with two seconds in this downpour, it would be back to being a curly mess. I surrendered to the ponytail holder in my center console, tying my hair up in a high bun to keep it away from my face for when it did inevitably decide to explode. My makeup still looked great despite the humidity – I sent a small prayer of thanks for the invention of waterproof liquid eye liner.

I reached to the backseat, grabbing my portfolio case, and struggled to fit the large folder on my lap while I mentally psyched myself up to run out in the rain. An umbrella would have been a wise choice, but definitely one I hadn't remembered to make.

Opening the car door, I sprinted to the door as steadily as I could in my heels – which I was certain was similar to watching a baby giraffe take its first steps at the zoo, but much wetter. I straightened my lucky blazer – blue velvet, vintage, got me at least four of my best clients – and raised my hand to knock, but the door opened before my knuckles could hit it.

I glanced up to see one of the most gorgeous women I had ever laid eyes on. Her short blonde hair was perfectly styled back in a way that showed off her sharp jaw. Her clear blue eyes seared into mine. Her tall, muscular body was covered in one of the most impeccably tailored button downs I'd ever seen in my life.

No way.

This could not be happening to me.

The woman in front of me was none other than Remington Van der Meer.

The wrong girl.

CHAPTER TWO

Remington

"Kelly, what's this appointment on my calendar for 3pm? Interior designer?" I spoke to the speaker across the kitchen. I was making myself another drink, slicing the peel of an orange with a paring knife in my hand.

"You need a change, Remington. We talked about this," the woman's voice was tinny across the granite counter. Hysterical that she still called me by such a formal title out of respect while making entirely disrespectful and inappropriate decisions, like hiring an interior designer.

I cringed, squeezing the orange peel, dropping it in the glass, and adding a generous dose of whiskey. "What I *need* is a little peace and quiet."

"You can have peace and quiet when you're not pushing for this deal."

I scowled at the speaker.

I had worked for years to get to the position of VP of Express Airlines. My father was the CEO and founder, but I'd proven I was more than capable of handling the job for years. Hell, I even did most of his job. The regional airport game wasn't a massive one, but we focused on mountain vacations and rural Midwest destinations — what others called Flyover Country.

Lately, I'd been pushing for Express to get involved in Southern destinations, so that we could rule the winter and summer, but my father hadn't been open to it. I'd even found a small airline, Osprey Airlines, with a profitable region that we had the potential to buyout. I just had to convince the Board, who generally looked upon me with favor since I'd busted my ass for the company for years.

Getting the Board in my favor meant that I'd have the control again, and that my father would have to listen to *me* for once. There were whispers about me replacing my father as CEO sooner rather than later, but I'd been a little too nervous for that step yet.

As it was, I was technically "taking some time" to be here in Colorado, though I was still working remotely on the deal. Just not my typical 12 hours a day.

Alison had been completely against any talk of over-ruling my father for reasons I had never understood until our divorce.

How many fucking times a day was I going to have to think about my ex-wife? My cheating, lying ex-wife.

"Well, if you listen to me, less fucking times a day," Kelly said. I jumped, raising a brow at the speaker. Had I spoken aloud or was she a mind reader?

"The former," she said again.

"Stop doing that," I said, feeling unnerved.

"Stop being so transparent and making it so easy," she scolded.

I smirked. Kelly, my executive assistant, had been by my side for nearly six years now. I had hired her because she reminded me of my nanny, and I didn't want to fuck her. Maybe I didn't want to fuck her *because* she reminded me of my nanny. Regardless, I didn't need distractions, and I didn't need to fuck the people I worked with.

The only downside was that Kelly knew me better than anyone, and so she frequently overstepped her bounds. Like this interior designer thing, for one.

During my divorce, she'd even found me a new apartment without me asking, simply because she knew I'd drag my feet and make myself miserable in the process.

I didn't want some snobby woman walking around my cabin and insisting that I needed florals and metallics and whatever else was in style right now. I just wanted this place to feel like home.

Nothing else did right now. I couldn't be in any of my properties without thinking of how Alison betrayed me. Her mark was all over them. She had never been to the cabin, though, despite having tons of her shit shipped here when I first bought it. That had surprised me, since she had been pissed when I bought the cabin in Breckenridge instead of Aspen or Telluride or even Vail.

Sure, we had separated eight months ago, and the divorce was final a month ago – thank god we never had kids – but I was a grudge holder above all else.

I had broken down and admitted to Kelly that I hated being reminded of anything ex-wife related, and that's why I had been working remotely from the cabin for a month. And of course, I had been feeling a little weird with the stress from the acquisition. Sure, I left out the part about not wanting to see another human being in the flesh, and maybe I should have emphasized that a bit more.

"Earth to VDM. Are you listening to me?" Kelly's voice cut through my thoughts.

"Fine, I'll give it a try. But no promises," I conceded, hanging up the phone with a quick bye. I checked my watch. 3:02pm. Late. First strike, design lady.

I saw the flash of headlights wash over the front of the house. Seeing as how I had purchased the most remote cabin I could possibly find, it had to be the design person..

I rolled up my shirt sleeves on my way to the door, ready to get it over with. I'd let her have a spiel and then I'd kick her out and be done with it. What would it take, thirty minutes? I bet I could do it in fifteen.

Nothing could have prepared me for who was standing on my porch.

In front of me stood one of the most stunning women I had ever laid eyes on. Her reddish-gold hair was pulled up out of her face, showing off a smattering of freckles across her nose and cheeks.

It was a face that was branded into my memory from a decade earlier. A face that I had never been able to forget, no matter how hard I had tried.

No way.

We stared at each other in surprise before I realized she was soaking wet and shivering.

Good. Let her be uncomfortable.

I leaned against the doorway, smirking, looking her up and down.

Julia Evans. I hadn't seen her since college, and she had grown up a bit since then. She had been an adorably awkward nerd back then, but she had filled out nicely in the years since. Her breasts were heaving against her silk camisole as though she had just run for her life, and her dark jeans hugged her full hips nicely. My jaw clenched as I imagined what it would feel like to grab those hips again, pull her tight against me. I remembered that first night, when we had snuck into the student lounge after hours…

"It's freezing," she said, interrupting my memory, crossing her arms across her chest.

"Yeah, looks like rain," I ran a hand casually through

my hair. In truth, the downpour had lasted a while and was showing no signs of letting up. The dark sky looked ominous, and the rain was loud enough that we had to raise our voices.

I still made no move to let her in, though. Why should I go out of my way to let this woman in after what she had done to me?

Had I mentioned I was really fucking good at holding grudges?

"May I come in?" She said through gritted teeth.

"By all means," I said, not stepping to the side.

She pushed past me, stomping into the foyer, setting her portfolio to lean against the wall as she shrugged out of her soaked blazer. I unashamedly stared at her round ass as she bent to pick the portfolio back up.

She stood, straightening herself. Her hair had begun to curl up around her temples, and I longed to untie the rest, feel it in my hands.

Goddamn, Remington, get yourself together.

She stuck a hand out to me, steeling her expression. "Nice to see you again, Ms. Van der Meer. I'm your interior designer."

Well, two could play at this game. I took her hand, clasping it and holding it, lightly rubbing my thumb over her knuckles.

A blush formed over her freckled cheeks. Good, then I wasn't the only one affected.

"How long has it been?" I said, casually, knowing damn well it had been ten years, five months, and give or take eighteen days.

CHAPTER THREE

JULIA

APPARENTLY I WAS THE ONLY ONE WHO KNEW OFF THE TOP OF my head it had been ten years. The last time I had seen her, she smelled like sex and she'd been begging me to start a life with her.

And now she was acting like we could be cordial?

Okay, asshole, whatever helps you sleep at night.

"Uh, Julia?" Remington said, snapping me out of my memories.

I looked her up and down for the first time since stepping into the cabin. Her shoulders had broadened, her jaw hardened. She had a slight darkness below her eyes, but they still shone bright blue, with a hint of gray. A pool on a cloudy day. Her hair was shorter now, not shaggy as it had been in college, but styled fashionably back, away from her face. I definitely did *not* notice how her shirt clung to her in all the right places, accentuating her small breasts and flat abs.

I crossed my arms over my chest once more.

Of course Remington would be as sexy as ever. Of

course she looked like she had a personal trainer while I had gained fifty pounds since seeing her last. We both looked better than ever.

Except, I had focused on what made me happy and she was divorced. So, I definitely still won the breakup.

A boom of thunder startled me, and I pushed my curling hair out of my face hastily.

Well, at least I wouldn't be dealing with Alison Dawes. Alison Van der Meer? I felt that familiar stab of jealousy. I had never even met the woman but of course I had stalked their wedding announcement and kept a Google alert for any birth announcements. None yet, though.

Call me a glutton for punishment. I had drawn the line at ever looking her up on social media, at least. Well, after the first year that I painfully stared at their Facebook pages and Twitter timelines for hours a day.

Above all else, I was a professional, and I wanted this project. So what if they'd cost me all the dignity I had left in the world? It would be worth it. It would look so good in my portfolio.

Wait. She had asked me a question.

I stared at her in silence, irritated all over again.

As if she could read my mind, Remington shrugged. "It's been awhile. Want to come in?"

She led me into the kitchen as she grabbed an Old Fashioned from the counter. Her hands held the chilled glass delicately, and I swallowed, remembering how those hands felt on my skin.

"I'd rather just keep this professional," I said, shaking my head to clear my memories.

She kept a perfectly blank expression, but nodded. "Alright, well, let's see what you can offer," she said, gesturing to my portfolio. I had the feeling she was going through the motions, not caring one bit what was inside the portfolio, eager to get me out of her life once more.

I cleared my throat, opening the case and pulling out my tablet, fabric swatches, pictures, paint chips. Some people worked completely digital, but I found that my clients responded better to something tangible, fabric and paint swatches they could trace their fingers over.

"Okay, well, your assistant mentioned that it would be kind of, uh, I believe her words were 'Bachelor pad,'" I said, stumbling over the word *bachelor*. It sounded so strange to call Remi a bachelor, gender implications aside. For some reason, it felt as though the word implied she'd be bringing women back there, and that thought made my stomach clench a bit with nausea.

I cleared my throat again, and she turned, filling a glass with water and handing it to me. "Go on," she said, moving around the counter to stand beside me.

I pointed to a picture of a sofa on the board, then gestured to the main open living space. "I'd love to hear what you think, of course, but these were my initial ideas." I glanced around, taking in the gigantic great room for the first time, which was completely unlike me. Normally I'd be checking it all out the second I stepped in, but I was just now looking around. Amateur hour. The space was nice, but… boring. Super boring. Not Remi at all.

Although, maybe I didn't know Remi at all, either.

"Now I'm thinking overall neutral tones as far as furnishings. Large pieces of furniture with soft, buttery, vintage leather, and we'll use pops of rich greens and blues to tie into the surroundings. And of course, I love this plaid fabric for accents." I paused, touching the soft fabric. "It ties in the deeper tones, but not overwhelmingly. Think throw pillows, blankets. Nothing over the top. It'll stay true to the... uh, masculine energy of the space," I hated saying it, but it was true.

Remi raised an eyebrow.

I turned, looking at the living room. The hardwood floors matched the wood trim, which matched the cabinets in the kitchen. It was way too 'Look at this log cabin' for my liking. I was excited that the walls weren't decked out in logs, though.

The centerpiece of the massive room was a three-story fireplace. It had gray stone, but it darkened the room a bit too much. The entire house seemed just a touch dreary. Boring and dreary. No wonder it was the perfect hermit cave.

"That fireplace is absolutely stunning, so I'd like to play off of that when it comes to paint colors. Would you be up for maybe a lighter wash on it to brighten up the room?"

Remi blinked, nodding.

I stepped away from her, taking a few steps towards the larger, main room. "The flow of this room from the kitchen feels kind of cut off, so if you're open to design instead of mere decoration," I pointed, my fingers itching for my measuring tape. I knew I was getting carried away, but I couldn't help myself. The space was stunning in person, and I was feeling inspired. "We could take out this wall and open up your kitchen into the main area, creating a larger feel that would match the expansiveness of the windows lining this wall and the fireplace over here."

I was holding up my hands, trying to envision lighting fixtures, when she appeared beside me. When I looked up, I could see that she was staring down at me with an intensity I recognized all too well. She was so close, and I could smell the orange on her, with a faint hint of chopped wood. It was so rugged, so consuming, I almost shut my eyes and leaned into her.

"Wow, this is impressive," she said, her voice deep and rich. Her eyes were hooded. She lifted her hands, reaching for me. "Jude, you... I—"

I startled at that. Her nickname for me. She was the only one that had ever called me Jude.

"Don't you dare," I said firmly, putting my hands out in front of me as a shield.

"Jude," she repeated, still looking as though she was intent on getting what she wanted. She put a hand on my shoulder, her thumb on my collarbone.

Ten minutes in and this was already happening?

The spell was broken. I clenched my hand into a fist to keep from slapping her across the face. She dared use her nickname for me *now*?

I thought I could stand it, but I was wrong.

I felt sick and trapped and I needed to escape.

I needed to escape every memory of how heartbroken she had left me. How I cried for months. Years. I had never been able to love anyone else. She had broken me, and I had spent years putting myself back together.

I didn't need her.

I pushed past her, walking as quickly as I could to the counter to grab my blazer. Forget the portfolio, she could have it. I just had to get out of there.

Years of heartache, years of longing for an answer, for closure, and this was what I got? Ten minutes in and she was just interested in getting in my pants again?

No, I wouldn't do it. I wouldn't rip open the scars that I had spent years carefully mending. A quick online search was one thing, but being in her presence was too much.

It hurt way too much.

Another flash of lightning sparked through the house, with a rolling boom of thunder close behind.

I had to leave. I had to get out of there before she made a fool out of me again.

"Julia, wait," she called, but I was at the front door, flinging it open and crossing the porch. The rain was pouring and the steps to the driveway were slippery and uneven. I prayed that my car wouldn't be stuck in the gravelly mud mixture pooling around the tires.

I glanced back once more to see her in the doorway, her arm over her head, leaning on her elbow, watching me go.

I got in the car, slamming my door shut. I wrenched the ignition a little too hard and turned the car around, thanking all the female patron saints I could remember that my car didn't get stuck.

The portfolio piece. The cash cow. I'd find another way to do it. I wouldn't sell my soul for a measly $10k.

I was capable and qualified and talented. There would always be more work. I careened down the drive, which was more of a meandering dirt road, honestly, but I stopped short at the bottom.

No.

No fucking way.

The bridge in front of me was completely washed out. The creek-now-river had overtaken it, fast-moving and out of control. The water was rough, sloshing against the eroded, muddy banks on each side. It looked like it had grown ten times its size, given how erratic the path and edges were. It was brown and murky, stirring up more than it should.

Okay, now I was projecting onto a river. *Get a grip, Julia.*

I inched the car forward, my stubbornness taking over all rational thought, thinking that maybe I could just push through it. I had seen enough car commercials to know that a Subaru could totally handle four-wheeling.

On a closed course with a professional driver, my rational side chimed in.

Well, sorry, rational mind. This was an emergency.

I knew I made the wrong decision the second my front wheels began sliding, the front of my car angling sideways. I had inched too far into the flooding area, and I was about to be swept away. Maybe if I just stayed very still… I gripped the steering wheel tightly, my heart pounding. The entire car began slipping, as though I was on an ice sheet.

Car commercials be damned, I knew how this would end. My death would be reported as some idiot reckless driver in the mountains who didn't respect Mother Nature enough to know to avoid flooding roads in the middle of nowhere.

I was *not* going down as a Driver's Ed cautionary tale.

I unbuckled, turned off the car, opened my door, and launched myself as far away from the flooding as possible, belly flopping in a display of sheer ridiculousness, I was sure. I landed in mud, but I was quickly pulled to my feet by strong, protective hands. I turned to see my car swept right into the flooding river. It twisted in the current, smacking into a tree about 50 yards down the path. I watched the airbags deploy, the windows suddenly white. *My car!*

I looked down at my mud-covered clothes. *My blazer!*

Priorities.

Not my finest first thought, but I was relatively unharmed. My dignity, however, was totaled.

"What the *fuck* were you thinking?" Remington roared beside me, soaking wet, cursing me.

"No," I shouted, shoving at her, blind and stupid with anger and memories and empty promises and her stupid attempt to do whatever she had been doing before I left.

I realized I was throwing a tantrum, but I couldn't get it together. I'd held it together for so long, and now? I just couldn't be near her. I couldn't face her after all that had happened. After what had just happened… My adrenaline was pumping and my hands were shaking.

"What were you thinking?" she yelled, holding my shoulders a bit harder than necessary, in my opinion. "You could have been killed."

"Let me go!" I yelled back, pushing at her, my dripping hair plastered to my face.

"And where will you go? With no car? No road?" She was bright red, *pissed*.

"*No!*" I yelled, again, powerless. I sank to my knees, totally overcome with pain in the moment. Sobs wracked my body. My shoes sunk into the mud, and the very dramatic side of me considered throwing myself to the ground and kicking and screaming. I was stranded with this jerk and nothing else but the memories of how heartbroken she had left me.

How long would I be stuck with Remington in that cabin – 5,000 square feet would still feel claustrophobic with her presence near me. I was shaking now, hysterically sobbing, unashamed of how wild I must look.

Remington waited a beat before kneeling in front of me. She pulled my hands away from my face, pushing strands of wet hair behind my ears. "Let's get back inside," she yelled over the sound of the rain, and lifted me up by the elbow.

My body was uncooperative, and my legs wouldn't hold my weight beneath me.

She bent to hook one arm behind my knees and the
other around my shoulders. She walked the path back up
to the house as I hung limp in her arms, afraid to hold
onto her, afraid to be alone with her, and afraid, more than
anything else, to be stuck here with her.

CHAPTER FOUR

REMINGTON

I DRAGGED JULIA INSIDE, KICKING THE DOOR SHUT BEHIND US. She was limp in my arms, as though she had exerted all of the energy in her body just to try to get herself killed and then scream at me.

I had never seen her so intense.

She was… shivering?

"You're okay, I've got you," I said, though I wondered what kind of comfort that might give her.

She had looked completely wild out there, screaming and hitting me. Unhinged, even.

But now? She looked small and frail and in need of my help.

I set her down on the bench in the entryway and held her cheeks in my hands.

"Are you cold?" I asked, assessing her ability to focus on me.

She blinked up at me, still shivering. "I… I think so."

I pulled her blazer off of her arms, then reached for the

edge of her camisole. "I'm going to get these wet clothes off of you," I explained, setting them aside.

She stared up at me as I did so, shivering violently. Luckily, she hadn't been out in the cold rain for long, so she couldn't have anything seriously wrong with her. I was more worried she could be in shock, though… I had seen it consume people before.

I grabbed a large scarf — more of a blanket, to be honest — from the coat rack and wrapped it around her shoulders.

"I'm going to lay you down now, okay?" I told her, and she glanced around, her arms wrapping around her stomach.

She didn't consent or disagree, though.

"Do you feel sick?" I asked.

She shook her head.

I gently pushed her down on the bench, lifting her legs slightly and holding her ankles. I took off her muddy boots and encouraged her to take deep breaths.

"Do you feel lightheaded?" I asked.

"No," she whispered, clinging to the scarf around her. She was still shaking, but her teeth had stopped chattering so violently.

Her wet hair fell down around her shoulders like a lion's mane. She still looked wild, but not in a terrifying way. In a strangely sexy way.

Here was a woman with a medical emergency and all I could think of was how sexy she was? I shook my head, tugging on her pant leg.

"We need to get these wet jeans off of you, okay? Can you unbutton your pants for me?" I asked, my throat going a bit dry and my stomach twisting at the idea of her unbuttoning those jeans while lying in front of me.

Medical emergency, Remi. Medical emergency.

She unbuttoned her pants and watched as I pulled them over her hips and knees, then reached to grab another warm scarf to lay over her legs.

She wiggled her toes, her brow furrowing. "Will I be okay?" She whispered, looking up at me with wide eyes. "Is it shock?"

I raised a brow at her question. Hadn't she been pre-med? "You'll be fine," I said. "It's probably just extremely mild shock. We need to keep you from fainting or anything worse," I said.

She nodded again, pressing her full red lips together in concentration.

"Can we at least lay by the fire where it's warm?" She asked, gripping the edges of the scarf around her shoulders.

"Do you think you can walk?" I asked, feeling a pang of worry.

"I think so," she said, lifting her feet out of my hands. She sat up slowly, steadying herself on the wall next to her. "Yeah, I can," she reassured me.

I held her elbow as she stood, the scarf I had laid over her legs falling to the ground. Her underwear were completely see-through and I tried my best to look anywhere else.

We walked over to the fire and she sunk into the couch. I grabbed a nearby blanket and covered her, placing her feet up on the arm of the couch to be above her head.

"Hey, Remi? Thank you," she said, grimacing slightly as though it pained her to say it.

I GULPED down the last of my second Old Fashioned, still glaring at Julia, as my worry over her condition eased. She sat on one of my barstools in a fluffy white robe, her hair wrapped in a towel, frantically trying to get cell service. At least we still had power, but I doubted that would last long.

After she had run out, I stayed on the porch watching after her car, feeling the loss of her immediately. I was pissed that she could still affect me like that, like it hadn't been any time at all, like the past ten years hadn't let me finally lay those feelings to rest.

I saw her brake lights a bit early, and that's when I spotted the bridge and the flooding just past her.

Well, fuck.

I waited for her to turn her car around, bracing to see her again. Maybe it would be easier when it wasn't a complete surprise.

That's when I saw the stubborn woman drive straight into the rushing water.

First rule of flash floods: don't drive your fucking car into them.

I didn't realize I was sprinting until I was on my way. I didn't realize I was terrified until I saw the car being pulled by the flooding and her car door open. My first instinct was that I'd throw myself into the water after her.

And when I saw her safely land on solid ground, my second thought was to shake her by the shoulders until her neck snapped.

I was shaking, so scared to have watched her almost be swept away. So scared to see how reckless she had been, how close she had come to danger.

I couldn't lose her again.

No, that was a bullshit sentiment. I hated her, but I didn't want her to die right in front of me.

I got it out of my head just as quickly as it had come in. There was no room for that kind of feeling any longer, not after what she did. I had carried her back to the cabin, making sure she didn't have hypothermia or shock.

After I had gotten her settled on the couch, she laid quietly for about an hour while I put her old clothes in the wash and found her a robe.

It wasn't until she had gotten up to take a shower that she had freaked out about the stupid blazer, though. If I remembered correctly, she had said there was no getting mud out of velvet, and I could have sworn she had quietly hummed TAPS under her breath as she had laid it on the drying rack in the laundry room.

Yep, she was still the same dork I remembered, but I found it way less endearing now.

I had made her take a warm shower, and in the meantime, cleaned myself up. I put on flannel pajama pants and a simple white undershirt.

I looked down at her bare feet, the slight swell of her calf, the small section of thigh that peeked out from where her legs were crossed. I absolutely did not notice if she was just as gorgeous as I remembered, that sun-kissed skin, the smattering of freckles wherever the sun touched. She was still the woman who had broken me.

I turned, reaching for the only thing I knew we could agree on without having to talk about.

I poured two glasses and slid one across the counter to her. No salt, no lime. I bought the good shit that didn't need it.

"I don't get any service here," she said, putting her elbows on the counter, holding her temples in her hands. "I'm stuck here forever."

I raised my eyebrows. I knew very well that cell service here was horrible, storm or no storm. That was half of the reason I bought the place. As for her being stuck, well, I wasn't that happy about it, either. I had come to the cabin to get away from cheating women. And there we were, her and I. No amount of panic over her wellbeing had brought her fully back into my good graces.

I was good at grudges, like I said.

She lifted her tequila glass to give it a sniff, then tipped it towards me.

"*Slainte*," I said, taking a sip. The sweetness bloomed on my tongue. I licked my lips, feeling the heat there, and saw that Julia was watching me intensely.

"Don't do that," she said, crossing an arm over her chest.

"Don't do what?" I asked, taking another sip.

"All of it," she said, gesturing to me with a grimace.

I stifled a grin. Well, this was a fun twist. Even if she had hurt me so long ago, toying with her now, making her remember how good she'd had it… well, the time stuck here together would be a little less dull.

To say it was an honorable plan would be a lie.

The lights flickered, and she jerked her head up. "Will the power go out?"

I shrugged. "Might." I had a backup generator, so I wasn't that worried.

"Do you have candles? Flashlights? Emergency rations? Water?"

"I think *somehow* we'll make it through," I said. Smirking, I slowly finished my tequila and poured myself another drink. Of course, I was prepared. *Was she?*

She tentatively sipped at the tequila.

I glanced at the clock. It was only seven in the evening, and I knew we had a long night ahead of us.

A FEW HOURS LATER, I could see that Julia was loosening up. Literally. She had taken the towel from her hair, and her robe had begun to fall open, and the freckled skin below her collarbone was visible. I was unashamedly watching to see if it'd slip down more. What could I say? She always had perfect breasts, and I wanted to know if they still looked like they had ten years ago.

What I wouldn't give to go back to those college years, to when we were raging with young hormones and couldn't get enough of each other. The things we'd tried…

My stomach stirred again.

"So why'd you get divorced?" She asked, her eyebrows raised.

Well, there went *that* nice memory.

"Way to just jump right in, Evans." I cleared my throat. I wasn't ashamed of my divorce — it was one of the best things that had ever happened to me. It just hit differently in front of Julia, and I felt more ashamed about the quick engagement, the marriage, and the divorce all at once.

Julia didn't even flinch.

"She cheated," I said flatly, swirling the honey-colored liquid around in the glass. Like all women did.

She nodded, her face blank. I'd have thought she'd at least have some kind of reaction, based on her past transgressions. I swore I heard her mumble, "That's what you get."

The lights flickered, then shut off completely, and I heard her gasp in the dark, the small sound pulling at something I'd buried deep inside of me long ago. The fire in the main room didn't give off much light over in the kitchen. I waited a few seconds for the generator to kick in, but I didn't hear it turning on. *Fucking great.* I wasn't about to go out in the pouring rain on a pitch black evening, a little drunk, in my pajamas, to see if I could get it working. That'd have to wait until the morning. It wasn't like we'd freeze to death in late August.

"Remi?"

Her voice was thin and quiet, and I could tell by her tone she was scared.

I rummaged under the kitchen sink until my hands landed on the flashlight and I used it to motion to the living room, where I'd lit a fire hours earlier for this very scenario, like some goddamned Boy Scout.

She led the way, sinking into the large couch closest to the hearth.

I added more wood to the fire and prodded it into place with the poker, leaning on my forearm over the mantle.

"This couch is really ugly, but it's comfortable," she said, wriggling back into the cushions.

"Well, maybe I'll just keep what I have and fire you." I smirked, setting my glass on the mantle.

"You're not going to do that," she said, shrugging.

"And why not?"

"Because I've got the perfect vision for this place," she said, shrugging.

This fucking woman. Hot and cold and hot and cold. I was getting whiplash from the moods.

I raised a brow, looking at her. "A little cocky." My voice almost surprised me, low and gravelly.

"Am I wrong?"

No.

Yes.

What were we talking about?

I didn't fucking know anymore.

She stared me down with an intensity that made my head completely clear of all rational thought.

It took me two steps to cross the space between us, bringing my lips to hers. My hands wove into her curls, holding her to me. She didn't even try to resist, her hands clutching at my chest. Her lips parted and my tongue claimed hers, our mouths tasting like tequila and citrus. Her mouth was just as I remembered, soft and pliable and warm. I pushed her robe open, roughly palming her breast. She moaned softly into my mouth, nipping at my lower lip.

I lowered her back onto the couch, moving to lick and nip at her neck as she made those soft moaning noises that made me so fucking turned on I could barely move. She pushed her hips into mine, the robe falling open at her waist.

I dragged my fingers over the soft skin of her hip, squeezing her ass in my hand.

She ground her hips into mine, and I could feel her heat against my leg. Dear Lord, grant me the patience and self-restraint to pull away, to tell her it wasn't right.

We fit together like we always had, like we were made for each other. I sunk my hand into those curls, pulling her head back further to expose the delicate column of her neck, nipping and sucking on her sensitive skin as she tipped her head back, biting her bottom lip, cooing as she thrust her hips harder into mine.

The lights flickered back on, startling us both.

"Wait, wait" she said, holding a hand to my chest as she breathed quickly. "No, no, no."

I sat back, giving her some space.

"That was… completely unprofessional of me," she said. "That was just nerves. I'm not—" Her eyes were wide with a kind of intensity I had never seen before.

"No, I—"

"I mean it. I have no idea what that was, but it's not happening again. We have it out of our systems, and now it's not happening again." She swallowed, pulling her robe tighter around her.

The lights turned back off just as quickly as they had turned on.

My mind reeled as I stood. I suddenly understood her urge to flee earlier, to put as much distance between us as possible. I turned in a circle, one hand on my hip as the other rubbed my face to gain some clarity back. "You want some pajamas?" I massaged anxiously at the back of my neck.

She nodded, rubbing at her eyes as though to clear her own thoughts.

I went in search of a pair of pajamas upstairs in my bedroom, taking my time as I took some deep breaths and splashed some cool water on my face. I gave myself a brief pep talk in a mirror.

Keep it the fuck together, Remington. Game face. Game face.

When I finally returned, I found her tucked into a ball, completely asleep.

She snored, turning onto her side, the robe lifting to reveal a perfectly round ass cheek. Her curly hair flew out from every angle, making her look young and carefree.

I sighed and raked a hand through my hair. I moved the robe back to cover her, though I did think for a moment it'd be a better view for the night if I didn't, and then grabbed the blanket I had wrapped her in just hours before and draped it across her body again.

I settled down on a chair near the fire, grabbing my tequila and a blanket for myself. She'd be scared if she woke up alone in the living room and I was upstairs in the bedroom, wouldn't she? It was honorable to keep watch.

She mumbled in her sleep, and I watched as she flung her arm out and turned onto her side, settling into the couch cushion. I remembered she had always been a wild sleeper, limbs and elbows thrown without care.

On the other hand, my ex-wife, Alison, had slept with no movement, so still I had wondered if she was dead once or twice. She had even bought a special pillow to remain on her back because of some bullshit about it causing less wrinkles on her face. Botox had also helped that, but then she hadn't been able to smile. Not that she did that much, anyway.

I hoped that wherever she was, she was as miserable as I was.

So close to what I had thought about constantly for a decade and so far from having it back.

The last time I had seen Julia, we were entangled in the back of her car, murmuring promises of what was to come.

And now?

I didn't know what I wanted.

Who knew when we were going to get her out of here so I could resume my life as normal? Or as far away from normal as I'd found, running a company remotely. And the first step was to stop staring at her as though she was a work of art.

She was just a woman. A fucking gorgeous woman whose body I had dreamed about for years, but a woman, nonetheless. And a woman who had wronged me in the past, and who would most likely wrong me again in the future. There were plenty more women in the world – isn't that what everyone had told me after the divorce?

Plenty.

I shifted in my seat, standing to go upstairs to my own bed. I had never been an honorable woman, and I wasn't going to start now.

CHAPTER FIVE

JULIA

I OPENED MY EYES TO A VERY WET SNOUT IN FRONT OF ME, slathering me in slobber. The dog smelled overwhelmingly wet and musty, and my stomach lurched.

I pushed the dog gently away and sat up slowly, trying to avoid throwing up.

My robe fell open, and I realized the belt was completely untied. Had I untied that in the night or…

No, that seemed low even for Remi.

I whipped my head around to see if she was in the room and immediately regretted that movement, bending over with a wave of nausea.

"Good morning, Sunshine," Remington said from the kitchen, holding a glass of orange juice and crossing the room towards me. "I know that McDonald's breakfast was your guilty hungover pleasure, but this will have to do."

I took the glass from her, pulling my robe tighter around me. I held my hair out of my face — I could only imagine the lion's mane situation that must be happening.

I pointed to the dog. "Who's that?"

Remington shrugged, scratching the dog's neck. "I'm not sure. I found her on the porch this morning, hiding out from the rain."

"It's *still* raining?" I said, glancing toward the large windows.

"Yep, still pouring. You should be glad this place is on the top of a hill. I can only imagine Breck is flooding, but we should be fine here for the time being. I did manage to get the generator working again this morning though," she said.

Rain meant that I was still stuck there. I groaned, leaning back into the cushions.

Oh no, I had forgotten to send Cam my location. She must be panicking, reading the news about flooding in the area.

"About last night—" Remi started, rubbing the back of her neck with her hand.

"I was all over the place yesterday," I said, shutting down the conversation. I was in absolutely no mood to recall the way I had basically torn off her clothes the second she'd gotten within arm's reach. Desperate, much? Maybe Cam was right about how me never sleeping with anyone was going to catch up with me. This was my punishment for all that pesky celibacy of the past few years.

She pressed her lips together, her brow furrowing. "Me too."

"Yeah, I..." I paused, recalling the dramatic events of yesterday, how I'd scrubbed mud out from places mud should never be. How she'd so expertly cared for me. Where the hell had that come from? "It's just a lot."

We sat in uncomfortable silence, watching the dog pace around the living room as I sipped at the orange juice.

"Do you have dog food?" I asked, glancing back to

Remi, who was leaning on the kitchen island. I noticed she was properly dressed and perfectly coiffed. It was inhuman how attractive she looked.

She shrugged, opening the fridge. "I have some frozen chicken and broccoli and rice… I guess this lucky little lady is eating gourmet for a day or two until we find her owner." She rubbed the dog's cheeks as she smiled down to her, cooing at her.

Any halfway normal woman watching would have had her ovaries explode at the sight. I looked away to avoid having any kindness in my being for her.

I didn't remember her as such a softy for animals. Then again, my memory had been pretty heavily leaning toward hatred for the past ten years, so it seemed only normal to forget the things I had actually liked about her.

My stomach grumbled, and I couldn't tell if it was due to nausea or hunger. Both? Tequila was weird.

"Want me to make breakfast?" She asked, pausing her cuddles with the dog.

"Uh, sure. Yeah. Scrambled eggs and toast? I can help," I said, finishing the juice and standing. My mouth was watering at the idea of the real food. I pulled the robe tightly around me, but not before I saw her watching it intently.

"Do you still like cheese in your eggs?" She asked, walking into the kitchen.

"How do you remember all of this?" I was annoyed by the remarks, pushing my hair out of my face again.

She shrugged noncommittally. She grabbed out the frozen chicken and tossed me a bag of rice. "For the dog," she explained, when I looked confused. Damn, she wasn't kidding about the pup eating gourmet.

The dog followed us into the kitchen and was sitting at my feet, licking her lips. I looked down to see two large, brown eyes looking sadly up at me. "Already a beggar, I see," I teased her, reaching down to scratch her big, blocky head. She was adorable, whatever kind of bully breed she was.

Remington was watching us when I looked up, and she looked slightly pained by the interaction. I only had a moment to wonder what her deal was until she started instructing me on how much rice and water to put in the cooking pot.

"I guess we'll boil the chicken, too?" She shrugged, looking down at the packaging. "I doubt she really has standards at this point."

"I wonder where she's from. And how she knew you were the biggest sucker in the neighborhood," I joked, smirking at Rem.

She dramatically put a hand on her hip, looking properly affronted. "So I'm a sucker just because I like dogs and don't want them to drown on my property?"

"No, you're a sucker because you are giving her frozen chicken when you have no idea how long we're going to be stuck here and what kind of reserves *we're* going to need," I said, rolling my eyes.

"Valid point," she said, pointing at me with the spatula. "Guess you only get one egg, if we're rationing." She proceeded to crack eggs into a bowl and add a splash of milk.

We resumed making breakfast with relative ease, but stayed out of each other's personal space, making sure not to touch. As we sat down at the breakfast bar, I scooted my chair to give myself a little extra room.

"So what's been new in your life?" She asked, piling her eggs onto her toast. I had seen her do that dozens of times before, and the pang of familiarity made my heart ache.

"Well, I'm an interior designer," I said with a small sweeping gesture toward the main room, avoiding the most obvious news.

"I was wondering about that. Weren't you pre-med?" She asked, shoveling more food into her mouth as though she'd never eaten and would never eat again.

I shrugged. "People change. Funny, that."

She cleared her throat. "Are you any good?" She asked easily.

"You hired me, after all." I grinned.

"My assistant hired you," she corrected, taking a large bite.

I paused, lifting my brows for a moment. Wow, the second I had started to see a different side of her, she reminded me she was still a rude asshole.

"Do you think we have cell service yet?" I asked.

She looked up towards the ceiling. "We didn't when I checked this morning, but you never know."

I reached across the bar to where my phone was, looking at the screen. Almost zero battery and still no service. I laid it back down, disappointed.

"Do you have any iPhone chargers?"

She glanced around, as if one might pop out at any moment. "I have an Android."

I grimaced.

"Are you one of those women constantly on their phone?" She asked, looking skeptical.

"No, I have an appointment today," I lied. I hoped Cameron hadn't already put out a Missing Person alert. Would Search and Rescue find my car and think the worst?

We ate in silence for a few more moments.

"What's new with you?" I asked.

Remi smirked. "Bet you'll never guess."

I nodded. Ah, right. We'd covered a bit of that the night before. "So, how do you know Alison was cheating on you?" I asked suddenly, looking up from my plate.

Her eyes widened, and she chewed the food in her mouth very slowly, as though she was contemplating what answer to give me.

"We, uh," she swallowed, pausing again as she took a drink of orange juice, clearly stalling. "Well, I walked in on it." She stared at me with an intense gaze that I couldn't read.

I cringed. "That sounds awful."

"Yeah, seems to happen to me a lot," she mumbled, standing and clearing her plate.

What was *that* about?

I stood, taking my own to the sink as well.

Projection much? Seemed a bit ridiculous, coming from a woman who never told me she was engaged.

The dog whined at our feet, pawing at my leg.

"Oh, we forgot her food," I said, pushing past Remi to get the rice and chicken off of the burner. I drained the water out of the pot, grateful for a task to keep from looking at her.

I had no idea what she was alluding to, but whatever it was, I didn't want to rehash it. We had an almost-nearly-slightly pleasant twenty minutes together, why ruin it now? I ran cold water over the chicken and rice to cool it down, and then placed it into a bowl, setting it on the ground.

To walk in on your wife cheating on you, though... I couldn't imagine. Even evil monsters like Remington didn't deserve that. "Did you know the person she cheated on you with?" I asked before I could hold back. I was impossibly curious.

She nodded, clenching her jaw. "Do you want a play-by-play?"

Well… yes, of course I did.

I thought about how good it would feel to know that the woman she left me for had hurt her, but I also realized that no amount of revenge would ever make me feel truly better.

Still, I had to admit to myself that something about hearing that Alison cheated on her made me feel a bit heartbroken. Maybe the memory of it happening to me? I had always been an empathetic person.

I brushed aside the feeling, knowing that if I looked too much into that, I didn't know where it would lead.

We stared at each other for a moment, and her eyes shifted to my robe, and the air charged around us.

No.

I walked out of the kitchen.

What we needed was a task that was not hot in any way. And I needed a change of clothes.

<hr>

Twenty minutes later, I was standing in the guest room wearing one of Remington's button down shirts and a pair of feminine sweatpants whose owner I did not want to consider. I looked like an idiot.

Unfortunately, my clothes hadn't made it through an entire wash cycle before the power had gone out, so Remington had offered a shirt that had shrunk in the dryer – yes, that *had* spurred on a three minute rant about her housekeeper, just in case her asshole ways were under question.

Even worse, my blazer was ruined. Had I shed a tear just for that? Yes, I did. And I didn't feel shame about it. It *was* lucky, after all. Although after this bad fortune, maybe it was best that it had met its doom. Its luck had clearly worn out.

I had to roll the sleeves to the shirt about ten thousand times before they were anywhere near my elbows and I could move my limbs, but otherwise, I was comfortable.

My hair, on the other hand, was now requiring its own zip code with its incredible ability to take over the world. I did my best to tie it into a bun, but I knew that no matter what I would try, nothing would make it look reasonable without a lot of product and a lot of time.

I tried to distract myself from the fact that the shirt smelled like her. How an unworn shirt could so vividly carry the leather and clove scent I had begun to associate with her, I had no idea. Maybe the bastard had sprayed cologne onto it before giving it to me.

"Are you ready or what?" She said, knocking on the guest room door.

No.

I hadn't been ready to see her face again yesterday, and I doubted I'd ever truly be ready to spend so much time in such close proximity with her again.

Now was not the time for that. I had a job to do, and I was going to do it, whether she liked it or not. I was stuck here after all, and I was going to use that to my advantage.

I arranged my best annoyed face and opened the door. "Someone's a little eager to redecorate," I said, pushing past her to walk down the hall towards the main room. She hadn't shown me the guest room last night, thankfully, on an entirely different wing of the house than hers, and I was upset that I'd slept on the ugly couch rather than the giant King size bed.

"Okay, let's start here," I said, standing in the great room again, holding the notebook I had asked her to find for me. The dog from earlier stretched out on the couch, sighing from lack of attention. "What do you envision using this space for, mostly?"

She looked blankly around the room, shrugging.

"Entertaining, relaxing, watching TV," I suggested, trying to get the ball rolling a bit.

"Definitely not entertaining," she said, stuffing her hands into her pockets. "Whatever is the opposite of entertaining."

"So, relaxing," I said.

"But no television," she quickly added, holding up a hand. "I hate TVs."

"I know," I said, stifling the urge to remind her that she did watch *The L Word* with me. She had claimed movies and TV were a waste of time when there were plenty of other fun things to do. Guess I missed that Here's-A-Pretentious-Jerk red flag originally. To be honest, I had only suggested it to seem like I *didn't* remember that bizarre fact about her. It was unnerving how much she remembered about me.

"Okay, so when you picture yourself relaxing, what does that look like?" I asked, knowing the question seemed silly, but my clients often gave me the absolute best gems in response to silly questions.

She furrowed her eyebrows, clearly out of her comfort zone.

"Are you lying on the couch, drinking whiskey, reading a book? What's your perfect evening?" I asked, walking around the living room. "Is there a fire? Is music playing? Are you all alone or is someone else here?"

I felt a shift in the air. Her eyes darkened, and I could only imagine what she was picturing.

I swallowed, pushing a curl out of my face.

For a moment, I thought she was going to cross the

room and take me in her arms again, maybe even rip my oversized shirt like some cover of a cheesy, 80s romance novel.

For a moment, I wanted that.

What was it about Remington? What *was* it that made me want to slap her across the face but also tear off her clothes and ride her until I shattered around her hands and mouth?

How could I despise her and still want her so intensely at the same time?

I shook my head, trying to release myself from whatever spell had taken over my body.

"I'm all alone," she said finally, her voice low as she rested her hands on the back of the couch and stretched her shoulders. "I'm reading a book or documents for work, and I'm drinking coffee or bourbon, but on a perfect night, I'm all alone. Always."

Her words sliced through me, cutting me to my core.

She was lonely? ...She could feel?

She didn't say it with a pitying tone, but I did detect some melancholy in her voice. Resignation, perhaps? Determination?

I scribbled *Comfortable, lounge* in my notebook and stepped away from the couch, willing myself not to think too much into it.

We walked around the main rooms of the house in much the same manner, deciding the ultimate purposes of each space until we reached the master bedroom. I was dreading this room with her, but at the same time, bedrooms were my absolute favorite spaces to design and I didn't get to do it often enough. Hence pining for the boutique hotel project.

I looked around the massive room, taking in the ugly oversized log bed, the small sitting area that lacked chairs just yet, and of course, the enormous bathroom that looked upsettingly gauche and straight out of an Italian villa. With marble everywhere, it screamed luxury. I scribbled in my notebook about needing to downplay all that marble so it'd look like something a human would actually use instead of just a nice bathroom from a catalog.

"Did you have this house built yourself?" I asked, running my fingers along the cool countertops, taking in the stone shower.

"No, I bought it from a friend," she said, leaning against the doorframe.

"Was your friend the Prince of Monaco?" I joked.

"No, just a Duke from Sweden," she said, furrowing her brow.

I whipped my head to look at her, trying to understand if she was serious. The corner of her mouth twitched. "Oh, you think you're funny, do you?" I laughed despite myself, rolling my eyes.

"I *know* I'm funny," she snorted.

I did a quick sketch of how the bathtub was laid out, trying to picture how I could calm the space down. Where the great room was boring, this bathroom could use a little more boring. I closed one eye, squinting with my other.

Remington laughed behind me, throaty and sinful. "Deep concentration, Ms. Evans," she said.

"Well, I want to get this right." I shrugged.

"What if we tore out everything in this bathroom, starting over?" She sighed, looking around. "I think this marble is ridiculous."

I lifted a brow. "It'd cost you more," I countered.

"What amount of money do you think it would take to

make this place truly perfect? Truly just mine?" She crossed her arms over her chest.

"I'd have to draw up some quotes and call around, and we'd have to sit down and talk to an architect to discuss if you want to change any of the layout," I said, my mind racing with ideas.

"What amount would I have to pay you to manage the entire project?" She stepped closer, trapping me near the shower.

"Like a General Contractor? Why?" What in the world was going on?

"Well, you're good at this. And I need this place." The intensity of her eyes made me take another step back.

I needed an absurd amount, anything to make her back up and give me some space. "One hundred thousand," I said quickly, almost without thinking.

"Done," she said, her eyes threatening to consume me whole if I wasn't careful.

Wait, what?

"You're going to pay me one hundred thousand dollars just to be your General Contractor? You'll pay for labor and materials on top of that?" I clarified. Did I have to tell her I have exactly zero experience managing a project of this size?

She nodded. "I trust you, Jude. You'll make it right."

I gulped. On the one hand, her using that nickname made me feel suddenly itchy all over. On the other, $100k? I wasn't sure where this trust was coming from, but it seemed entirely misplaced.

$100k?! That would pay off my student loans, be a downpayment on a house of my own, and pay for me to take on interesting projects without having to worry about the cost as much. Not to mention how incredible this mansion would look in my portfolio. I'd be able to land huge jobs from this one project. My mind raced with possibilities.

"You're honestly serious?"

Remington pulled her phone out of her pocket, swiping at the screen. She held the phone to her ear and spoke to someone named Kelly.

Oh, Kelly, the assistant I had spoken to before. She was talking quickly about a contract and a lawyer and…

She was serious?

I stared at her, gulping loudly. I had some small hint of an idea of what I was getting myself into, but at the same time, some small voice in the back of my mind screamed that I'd be regretting this choice. I'd have to work with *her*. I'd have to be around her. Did I really dare do that? After what happened last night?

I watched as she ended the call and stared at the phone in her hand. Something clicked inside of my brain and I quickly realized that she had just spoken to someone on the phone. How did she have service?

I held up a finger to her to wait and ran out of the room, racing down the stairs as fast as I could. I found my phone and held it up, my heart sinking when I saw that it was dead. Oh, right, the charger.

"Here, use mine," Remi said from behind me, making me jump.

I turned, seeing that she was standing with her phone in her outstretched hand. "Um, thanks, I'll just be a minute," I said, typing in Cam's number as I walked down the stairs into the main room to find the dog still snoring on the couch. Spoiled already.

I listened to the phone ringing, staring out the windows. The rain had let up to a soft drizzle, and the midday light was gloomy and dull.

"Uh, hello?" Cameron said with an irritated tone.

"Cam, it's Julia. I'm alive," I said quickly to cut off her panic.

"Where the fuck have you been? I was literally just about to call a search. You didn't send me a pin and you haven't answered the thousand calls or texts since."

I felt a pang of guilt. "I know, I'm so sorry. Listen, I'm stuck at this client's house, but I'm okay. I'm actually calling you on her phone."

"The divorcee?" Cam's voice turned chipper. Shameless.

"Uh, yeah, something like that."

"Is she hot? You gonna get a sugar mama?"

"She's…" I heard the stairs creak behind me and turned to see a curious Remi walking down them again. "It's all fine. I'm fine."

I could envision Cameron's skepticism. "Mmmhmm, yeah, when you're fine you definitely always repeat that sentiment ten times. Yep."

"You're breaking up so badly," I lied.

"Sure, honey. Okay, well, I'm glad you're alive, and I think there's some kind of story I'm not getting here, so I'm ready for that whenever you are." She laughed.

"Mmhmm. 'Kay."

"I love you, be good." She at least sounded sincere in her sentiment.

I paused, knowing Remi would hear me. "I love you, too."

I hung up the phone, looking down at it in my hands.

"Everything okay?" Remington called from the kitchen. She had started to busy herself with dishes while I was on the phone, giving me the illusion of privacy.

I nodded, twisting the phone in my hands.

"I guess I can call roadside assistance about my car now?" I called out, keeping my voice steady.

"Good luck with that," she said, her back to me.

"Why? You're not done holding me hostage just yet?" I leaned back on the couch, trying to search for local tow truck companies. I clicked the first one that loaded at long last. They informed me it'd be a week before they were able to help, due to all of the damage and it not being an emergency.

What about this wasn't an emergency?!

I hung up the phone in a huff. A week being stuck with Remi sounded like six and a half days too many.

"I'll need to call someone to repair the bridge before we can get out, anyway," she said, shrugging and leaning against the counter.

An email dinged on her phone, a message from Kelly with the design contracts. "Wow, she's fast," I said, holding out the phone, feeling jealous that she could get an email.

She crossed the room, taking the phone from me. She was silent as she flipped through the screens, reading intensely.

"Deep concentration, Ms. Van der Meer," I teased, repeating what she had said to me earlier.

In truth, my heart was threatening to beat out of my chest. I was so nervous about signing that contract.

"Can we lay some ground rules before I sign that thing?" I asked, twisting my hands in my lap.

"Like?" She said, barely lifting her eyes to me.

"Like are you going to pay for my lodging?" I crossed my arms over my chest.

"You'll stay here," she said, like it was obvious.

"No, I want my own space," I pushed back.

"You'll waste time each way getting here. It doesn't make sense for you to not stay here," she said, rolling her eyes.

"If I stay here—"

"Which you will—"

"We keep this strictly professional. You keep those bedroom eyes to yourself. Stop trying to sleep with me," I said, giving her a pointed look.

"Define 'try,'" she countered, lowering the phone, her interest clearly piqued.

"I mean it. Strictly professional," I said, standing from the couch.

"Alright, alright," she said, holding up her hands in surrender.

I didn't believe her.

"For the record though, you made the first move," she murmured, grinning.

"I did not!" I protested, feeling a bit outraged by the accusation. "*You* kissed *me*."

"Kissing is harmless," she said, rolling her eyes. "You reached under my shirt."

"I did not," I said, though to be honest, I couldn't exactly remember.

She raised her eyebrows. "Oh yes, you most definitely did. I can give you every detail of what happened last night, in fact. First, I kissed you. Then, we laid down on the couch. You're short and I didn't want you to strain your neck, you see. Then, I reached inside of your robe and twisted your—"

I held my hands up. "I get it," I said quickly, interrupting her replay. My heart pounded and heat stirred low in my belly. "You don't have to—"

"And then, you did that little whimper thing that drives me crazy, and arched your back, pushing your wet pussy into my leg, begging me," she continued, rounding the couch to come closer to me.

"I said strictly professional!" I said, stepping to the other side of the couch, away from her.

She laughed, biting her lower lip. "It would just be a pity for you to not remember last night, that's all," she said, shrugging.

I threw a pillow at her, my brow furrowed in indignation. The dog barked, jumping up, thinking that we were playing.

"This is the opposite of professional," I said, rounding the corner of the sofa as she pretended to chase me.

"Oh, I don't know, I've always enjoyed mixing business and pleasure." Did she really growl as she said that?

We paused and stared at one another, and I could see that her chest was heaving like mine was. There was total silence, save for the soft rhythm of our inhalations and exhalations. Even the dog was quiet as she looked between us expectantly.

My body was on fire for her, and at the same time, I was completely frustrated that she was toying with me like this. I shouldn't want her. She was the absolute last woman I should want. And yet...

"The rain stopped," she said, breaking my gaze.

We both turned to the windows, watching as the sky began to lighten. That was Colorado in a nutshell — flooding monsoon one moment, birds chirping in the sunshine the next.

"Do you think it's safe to venture out to my car?" I asked, getting an idea.

"It's not drivable," she said with a small chuckle.

"I left my laptop in there, and I have my fingers crossed it's still usable. I could start on the design plans here while we wait for the bridge to be repaired, at least," I said, starting for the door. I opened the closet, searching for some kind of boots. Tall snow boots — those would do.

"Wait," she said, following me. She grabbed muck boots out of the back of the closet and pulled them on.

I looked her up and down, trying to suppress a grin. "You look ridiculous in those."

"Yeah, and you look super cool in that getup, too," she said, waving her hand toward me.

I looked down at myself, seeing snow boots, sweatpants, and an oversized men's shirt. "I don't know, I think I'm really pulling off a cool new fashion here," I said, gesturing to my outfit grandly. "I am an *artiste*, non?"

She snorted, shaking her head. "You are so weird, Jude," she said with a grin, grabbing a couple of light jackets.

We put them on and started out the door. The dog walked between us as we stepped onto the porch. The air was chilly, but thick with humidity – a rarity for Colorado – and I was grateful for the jacket.

"It's probably still not very safe to get to your car, but we'll try," she said, navigating the muddy drive.

We stopped at the edge of the creek, assessing the situation. The bank was pretty steep, having washed away with the water. My car was about fifty feet downhill, still crushed against a tree. At least it was on this side of the creek. I felt a small shiver at the memory of having to jump out of it before it dragged me down with it.

Remington looked over the bridge, trying to determine how much was damaged and what would be needed for repairs. For a temporary fix, she explained, she could lay down boards so that we could at least drive across it.

The idea of freedom was bittersweet. I desperately wanted to get away from here, but despite her teasing, I had been having a not-too-terrible time. Sure, I felt dizzy and heated whenever she was near, but I was genuinely enjoying our banter, too. I had forgotten how easy it was to joke around with her. It was one of the first things that had drawn me to her. I watched as she picked her way down the bank towards my car, the dog following close behind her – the creek was still swollen and fast-moving, but it didn't seem as treacherous today, thankfully. I could see the perfect curve of her tight, muscled shoulders through her light jacket, and my hands itched to touch her again.

No. Strictly professional. $100k.

I inhaled deeply, trying to clear my mind of the images of what I found myself desperately wanting to do to and with and *for* Remington.

Focus.

I walked down along the bank, following the path she and the dog had taken. I held my hands out for balance, slipping in the mud slightly, but overall, I didn't feel unstable.

We made it to the car and wrenched open the backseat door, the only one that looked like it would open. My satchel bag still lay across the backseat, holding my notebooks and laptop. It felt like treasure to get my hands on it again.

I heard a scuffle behind me and turned in time to see the dog sliding down the bank, her limbs flailing to find purchase against the muddy walls.

Remington shouted in surprise, scrambling down after her, finally landing on her ass to lower her center of gravity in order to not fall after the dog.

The dog whimpered, her eyes wide with terror as she caught her front legs on a fallen tree limb wedged into the mud. The water was rushing just below her back feet.

"I can't reach her," Remington said, panic in her voice.

I tossed my bag down, scrambling after them. It was

my fault we were out here, and if anything were to happen to this poor, helpless creature… I didn't want to think about that. Right now, we just needed to save her.

"Grab my hand," I said, reaching for Remington. "You hold onto the tree. I'm not strong enough to pull you both up, but you're strong enough to get us. I'll try to reach her," I explained, locking my fingers in hers.

The tree branch shifted under the dog's weight and she whined in fear.

"It's okay, baby, we've got you," I cooed to the dog. If she began to panic, she'd dislodge the branch altogether and I'd have to jump in the water after her. I wanted to avoid that at all costs.

"Be careful, Jude," Remington said as I reached, trying to will my arms to be just a bit longer as I tried to grab the dog. She was just out of my grasp.

"Hold my ankle," I demanded and twisted onto my belly to get closer. Remington's hand wrapped firmly around my leg and I slid towards the dog, finally able to grip her scruff enough to pull her towards me. She was a sturdy little dog, but not exactly easy to lift.

"You're okay, baby girl," I cooed, dragging her up the bank and into my arms. I wrapped my arms around her chest and she struggled against me, still afraid. I stilled, trying to use a soothing tone to get her to calm down.

I heard a strange creaking noise, almost a metallic groan, and turned my head just enough to see my car slowly beginning to slide down towards us. We must have shifted it just enough when we opened the door.

Remington had heard it, too, and was frantically pulling on my leg. "Jude, get up, get up," she yelled, the muscles in her arms bulging.

Time seemed to stand still. Pure adrenaline coursed

through my veins and it felt as though everything happened in the exact same moment – I lifted myself onto my knees, holding the dog in my arms. Remington whipped us back against her and we huddled against a tree together while my car crashed down the side of the creek, falling sideways into the water where the dog had just been.

Where I had just been, too.

I felt like I was out of my body, watching an action movie happen in front of me. It took me a moment to realize that I was crying in sheer panic, clutching the dog to my chest. Remi held us both against her, her arms enveloping us. She shushed into my hair and the dog panted and struggled, probably feeling just as much terror as I was.

"We're fine," Remington said against my ear. "I've got you, we're fine." She repeated this in the same soothing tone I had just used on the dog, but it was working.

The dog scrambled out of my arms, climbing up the bank to safer ground. She shook her coat and looked back at us, expectant.

"Are you okay?" Remington said, holding the sides of my head in her hands and staring into my eyes.

I nodded, my eyes feeling as wide as dinner plates. "You saved us." My voice cracked.

"I just dragged you. You mostly saved yourself," she said, shaking her head.

I was shaking, but feeling much less like I would go into shock than 24 hours before.

She turned, looking to where we'd have to climb. "Come on," she said, reaching again for the tree and pushing me up the bank. I crawled on my hands and knees, getting to a slightly more solid ground before turning to reach for her and grab onto her forearm as she climbed up behind me. I reached down for my satchel — it had miraculously been unscathed in the final, dramatic death of my car — and we trudged in silence back to the house, the dog leading the way.

CHAPTER SIX

"WELL, NOW WE HAVE TO NAME HER," I SAID AS WE STRIPPED off our mud covered boots and jackets on the porch.

"Oh, really?" She said skeptically, untying the laces of her absolutely disgusting snow boots.

"Yeah, I mean, after that, we're bonded," I said, feeling a bit like it was just common sense. After what we had just gone through… my panic at losing the dog was nothing compared to my panic about losing Julia. Seeing her sliding down the bank of the river after the dog surely took ten years off my life. That was two times in two days I thought I had lost her.

No, Remington, get it together. She's not yours to lose.

She laughed, rolling her eyes. "How about River?"

"Too obvious," I said, tapping my chin in thought.

"Brook," she said, smirking. "Rio."

I shook my head. "No, that's a male name."

"Like it matters," she muttered, wiping her muddy hands on the sweatpants I had given her that morning. "I don't think dogs really have gender identities, Remi."

"She needs a good name!" I said, feeling a bit affronted.

"Stormy," she said, throwing her hands in the air.

I paused for a moment. "I like that."

We both looked down at the dog. "What do you think, Stormy?" She asked. The dog sat up straighter, wagging her tail. Her mouth split into a giant grin.

"Well, that settles it," I said, walking through the front door. I unbuttoned my muddy pants, sliding them over my hips, when I heard her gasp. I turned, seeing her in the doorway, staring at my hands.

She quickly held her hands over her eyes. "Don't undress here," she said, shaking her head.

What, like the neighbors would see me?

"You've seen me in much less, Evans."

She turned her back to me, shaking her head. "That was then," she said, her hands on her hips.

She was right. That *was* then. But now? As much as I wanted to hate her, I just… didn't? I couldn't. She had betrayed me at my most vulnerable. I had plans to propose and have our life together. I had to remember that, so that I could stop swooning over her like a teen girl.

Seeing her standing in my shirt, however muddy and gross it now was, did give me a light, warm feeling, though. No words could explain how I felt — pulled in two completely opposite directions. What had happened was heartbreaking and life-ruining, but now? Now I felt like I could grab her in my arms and make her mine. Like I could make the promises I had once before.

I shook my head, taking my hands away from the buttons of my pants.

What had come over me, offering her an obscene amount of money to redesign the house?

Julia made me reckless, and I couldn't afford to be reckless right now.

Not when I was running my father's company, not when I was in the position of convincing the Board to trust my opinion over his. I had to focus.

"I'm going to go shower," I muttered, walking down the hall and up the stairs, to my bedroom.

The idea of losing Julia like that, of watching her be crushed by her car, had damn near wrecked me. I couldn't be distracted. I had to put some distance between us.

Twenty minutes later, I sat with a towel tied around my hips, standing in my offensively overdone bathroom as I combed my hair. Having it redone was the right choice, but choosing Julia for the project? I rubbed at my eyes, willing my sanity to come back.

I liked her vision. That was all. She had a good vision. It was nothing more. It was absolutely nothing more.

There was a knock at the door. "Come in," I said without thinking, combing my hair.

"Oh, I… uh…" Julia stood in my bedroom, staring into the bathroom where I was. Her eyes were on my towel, and I could almost feel her gaze over my small breasts, the slight V cuts of my hips. "I didn't mean to…"

I suppressed a smile. "What?" I asked casually, trying my hardest to look like I was a bit annoyed with her. Instead, my lower belly tightened at the sight of her messy curls. She had taken off the muddy sweatpants and shirt and stood in the robe from last night. Goddamn, she was so sexy without even trying.

"I was just wondering if you were done with the shower. I just gave Stormy a bath, and, uh," she said, furrowing her brow and staring intently at my face.

I leaned against the doorway of the bathroom, having a

bit of fun with the idea that she found me just as attractive as I did her.

"Sure," I said with a small lift of my shoulder.

She turned to go, but stopped. I could tell she was trying to work herself up to tell me something by the way her lips were pressed together and how she was wringing her hands. "Hey, I just wanted to thank you," she said slowly.

I tilted my head.

"For… saving me," she continued.

"Sure," I said, maintaining my composure, even though every part of my being begged to wrap her in my arms and tell her how scared I was that she might have been hurt. I settled for clearing my throat and standing up straight. "It's not like I could have let you die. It'd really weigh on my conscience," I added, rubbing at the back of my neck. "And I needed you to save Stormy."

Her eyes widened as she stared at my chest and shoulders. "Y-yeah," she stuttered. "I'd hate for you to feel guilty about letting some lady and dog die on your property."

I smirked. "With my luck, you'd both haunt the place."

"You're damn right I would. You thought Poltergeist was bad? Child's play," she said, grinning mischievously.

We stood in silence for a moment, looking each other over. The air grew thick around us, and I could tell we were a moment away from ripping each other's clothes off. Well, what little left we were wearing. Even if she did smell a bit like wet dog. My standards were fairly low at the moment, apparently.

"You can use this shower if you want," I said, hooking my thumb over my shoulder to point to the one in my bathroom.

"Thanks," she said, looking past me. "I think I will. Looks fancy as hell."

I pushed past her, directing her to which bathroom cabinet held the towels. She walked into the bathroom and shut the door behind her.

I was probably in need of another shower from the moment, and the idea that she would be naked and wet in my shower didn't help that at all.

Just as I was considering the idea of opening the bathroom door and joining her in there, Stormy started barking downstairs. I sighed, grabbing sweatpants and a t-shirt out of my closet and slipped them on, using the towel to continue drying my hair as I walked down the stairs.

Storm had her full hackles up and was barking at my phone ringing on the kitchen counter.

"Wow, you're some guard dog," I teased, rolling my eyes. My mother's picture popped up on the screen.

I tossed the towel on the barstool, then scratched Storm behind the ears as I hit the green accept button.

"Hi Mom," I said, opening up a cupboard to find what we could make for lunch.

"I've been worried sick," she started in her thick Southern drawl.

"Yeah, the rain is pretty bad. My property has a river now. Do you think that increases the value?" I found a box of orzo in the pantry and a jar of pesto with the canned goods. Did we have any frozen veggies?

We?

Ugh, get a grip, Rem.

"Don't joke with me, young lady."

It always threw me off that my mom thought of me as young or a lady, when I'd been dressing in clothes from the men's section for decades and my hair had already started to turn gray. Maybe I needed to step up my retinol game. Was 33 too young to launch into an aging skincare regime?

"I'm okay, Mom. Really. The generator is working and—"

Stormy barked again about something, wagging her tail. Was she seriously barking about thunder?

"Was that a dog?"

"Oh yeah, we found a stray dog," I said, reaching down to pet Stormy.

My mother sighed. I could almost picture her look of exhaustion. "I heard a rumor," she began.

Well, that sounded ominous. I stayed silent, waiting for the dramatics to give way to the actual information.

"Something about convincing the Board of a potential buyout?" She began. My mother owned 20% of the company after her parents had passed, giving her — and only her, not my father — their shares.

"I'd love to talk about that when I have better service," I started, knowing it'd be a longer conversation.

"Alright, dear, I look forward to that. For now, I have to get going. Your father has an event tonight, and the stylist finally arrived." Her tone shifted slightly. "Nearly an hour late."

Wow, was that what I sounded like when I complained about Julia being late? I grimaced.

"Stay safe, darling."

I sent her my well-wishes. My parents had been separated for nearly a decade. They'd started living apart shortly after I'd married Alison. Interesting timing… Now they operated more as business partners.

My phone rang again and I clicked the accept button without thinking.

"Everything okay?" Kelly asked before I could even get a hello in.

"Yeah, why?" I said, a bit confused.

"Well, first you asked for that contract, and then you didn't answer my calls for an hour," Kelly said, sounding a bit like my scolding mother.

"I was rescuing the damn designer from certain death, sorry," I smirked, leaning against the counter. "The contract come out okay?"

"You're sure you want to pay her this much money?" Kelly asked, the concern apparent in her voice.

"Yes."

No.

I rubbed my hand over my eyes. Ugh, I was a damned fool.

"Yes, you are," she said, though I could tell she was either smiling or hiding a silent laugh.

Even with bad service she could still read my mind. It was amazing.

My stomach growled and I stood, walking to the freezer to find veggies. Instead, I found a pizza and pulled it out, looking at the cooking directions, wondering if Julia liked green peppers. I remembered she hated olives…

"Remington Van der Meer, are you listening to me?" Kelly interrupted.

"Of course," I lied, turning on the oven.

"I have an update about the Board considering the Osprey buyout," she said. Wow, word had travelled fast. I wondered if my mother had anything to do with that. "Your lawyer wants you to hear it directly from him but I thought you may want to hear it from me, instead."

I had a bad feeling about her tone. "What?" My voice was a bit rude, but I couldn't help it.

"Word is that Osprey is already considering an offer from Guardian," she said.

Guardian was one of our biggest competitors… how

did they even know Osprey was exploring their options? Unless my father had something to do with it.

"That's vague," I said, ripping the cardboard box around the pizza.

"The details are still very vague, Remington," she snapped.

I felt a bit guilty, realizing that this stressed her out nearly as much as me.

"Trying to get back into the Southern market, too, I'm assuming?" I said, holding the phone between my shoulder and ear as I moved the toppings around on the pizza.

"Something like that," she said with a sigh.

"Do you think we can get the Board to move more quickly?" I asked, setting the pizza down to finally fully consider what she was saying. If we were going to stop this, we were going to have make a decision sooner rather than later, and I wasn't sure I felt comfortable. The thought made me cringe, but not nearly as badly as the thought of losing the purchase and the trust of the Board.

"I'm not sure, especially with you being in Colorado" she said quickly. It was clear that she had already considered this as well. "Can you make it back tomorrow?"

I looked out the window at the pouring rain. "Nope." Disappointment sank hard in my stomach. "Can we have Mike work his magic in any way? Make it seem like the Board's idea?"

Mike was the one of the Board members I actually trusted.

"Okay, I'll have Mike see what he can do here," Kelly said.

"Thank you, I appreciate you deeply," I said.

"As you should, VDM."

I wrapped up the conversation and turned around,

jumping a bit when I saw Julia standing at the counter, wearing another pair of Alison's yoga pants and one of the old t-shirts I'd had since college.

"Is everything okay?" She asked, and I could tell she was trying to remain casual.

"Yeah, just business," I said, busying myself with putting the pizza in the oven. My blood was boiling. Had my father somehow sabotaged this? Did we have a leak? It felt as though I was looking through fogged glass — no matter how much I tried to peer in, something was being hidden from view. I slammed the oven door shut and Julia flinched beside me.

"Seems like everything's totally fine," she remarked, crossing her arms.

"Why do you even care?" I asked, throwing my hands in the air.

Her eyes widened and she retreated to sit in the living room, Stormy following close behind her. She sat down on the couch and Stormy curled into her side.

Sure, I was being an asshole, but everything was going wrong. I couldn't help it.

I didn't expect the damn dog to pick her side, though.

CHAPTER SEVEN

Julia

"Okay, now, Gray Wisp or Gray Owl?" I held up my paint samples, showing Remi the two.

She stared down at them, her eyebrows pulling together in concentration. "They're... both definitely gray. I don't get it. They're literally the same color." She bit her lower lip, looking up from the paint deck, blinking.

I laughed at her joke, then paused when I saw her sincere expression. Oh no, she wasn't joking. She sincerely couldn't tell the difference between Gray Wisp and Gray Owl? They couldn't have been further apart. Gray Wisp was significantly darker, with much stronger green undertones. Gray Owl was absolutely in the "Griege" territory. I knew that they would both compliment the warmer undertones of the stone fireplace.

We sat on the couch, my computer on my lap, rendering examples of the great room for her approval. Stormy lay on the other side of Remi, stretching to take up a significant portion of the couch.

"Okay, let's try this again," I said, flipping open the

paint deck. Maybe if I showed her one of the gray examples versus a color that wasn't similar, she'd be able to imagine it clearer. I held up Van Courtland Blue and Gray Owl.

She looked back and forth between the two samples. "I don't like this. I feel dumb, like I'm failing a test. I know one is blue and the other is gray, but I just don't see much of a difference here." She leaned back on the couch. "And honestly, I don't really fucking care."

I pointed to the massive wall. "When you have three stories of Gray Wisp, I don't want you sitting here thinking, 'If only I'd gone with Bunny Gray.'"

Remi blinked, her eyes wide as she stared at me. "I hear the words coming out of your mouth, I understand all of them separately, and yet, it's like you're speaking an entirely different language. Really Jude, I couldn't care less what gray you choose."

My chest clenched at the nickname, and she seemed to realize her mistake.

She looked away and took a long pull of her cocktail, some kind of Paloma-ish drink she'd made up that went down a little too easily.

I'd spent the afternoon working diligently on my plans for the room, including ideas for the redesign. I knew some annoying architect would try to talk me out of some of the ideas, thinking I couldn't possibly be as well-informed as I definitely was, but I was ready to put up a fight for some of my better plans.

"What made you want to go into interior decorating? I honestly thought you had such a passion for doctoring." Remi looked at me with a kind of intensity that had once made me weak in the knees. Now it just made me feel like I was in over my head.

"Uh, well... I just needed a change." Not a lie, but a definite understatement.

"You didn't come back to school after Spring Break." She bit her lip again, staring down into her glass.

I nodded, pressing my lips together. Why did she even care? "I never went back."

She looked startled by the admission. "You never finished?"

Shame swirled in my stomach, and I could feel my cheeks growing warm. God, I wished we were talking about Bunny Gray. Hale Navy. Hell, I'd even take Blue Spruce at the moment.

"I just realized I maybe wasn't actually that passionate about being a doctor." Another understatement. After she broke my heart, I didn't feel passion for *anything* that had once interested me. I needed a subject change—fast, before I either punched her in the nose or tried to leave again. "Where did you learn how to treat someone about to go into shock?"

I remembered feeling so comforted by her confidence after the initial terror had worn off, almost relieved that I was with her instead of anyone else. She made me feel so safe in that moment, and that was dangerous. That feeling led to our kiss the night before—a complete mistake that I wasn't willing to make twice.

She lifted a shoulder and I half-expected her to dodge my question, but after a long pause, she spoke. "I took a wilderness first responder training." She watched me over the rim of her glass as she took another sip.

I tried to hide my confused expression. Since when had Remi ever thought of anyone but herself?

"Why?" I asked, setting my laptop down on the coffee table. I picked up my drink, swirling it around in the glass.

She shrugged. "I was going to hike the Colorado Trail,

and I wanted to be able to take care of myself or anyone else I found along the way who might be in need of help." There was an edge to her voice that I recognized immediately—there was more to that story.

"A lot to unpack here. Since when do you long-distance hike?" I asked. "Because I remember trying to hike Quandary with you and you were a mess." I laughed despite myself at the memory of her screaming when one of Quandary Peak's famous goats crossed our paths. She had already thrown up from altitude sickness about a mile in, but refused to let our group turn around. I wanted to strangle her, and then the goats made her think she was hallucinating.

I could see a grin tug at the edge of her mouth. "Okay, first, I remember someone giving me quite a lot of whiskey the night before, and second, there were *killer goats*." She raised her eyebrows, as though challenging me to question her memory.

I shifted in my seat, angling my body towards hers. "Killer goats? You mean the fluffy, white, adorable goats who just wanted to trot alongside us and eat Cameron's trail mix?"

"Wow, way to be a Killer Goat apologist, Julia." Remi shook her head as though she was deeply ashamed of me.

"Okay, I'm sure that absolutely happened and I'm just misremembering it, of course. But, what the hell made us drink whiskey the night before?"

"Cameron, of course." She rolled her eyes. "It was her birthday. That's why we hiked Quandary at all."

Cameron as a college roommate was a lot less responsible than Cameron as a best-friend-slash-motherly-influence. She had seen me through the worst of it, and even though I hadn't gone back to school after the Remi breakup, she had still made it a point to stay in touch, so our friendship had stayed strong. She was a good egg. A terrible 22-year-old influence, but a good egg now.

"Yeah, that sounds about right," I said, smirking. "I wonder what she'd say if she knew I was here. She knows I'm somewhere out here, but she doesn't know it's with you."

Remi glanced at her phone. "Is *that* who you were talking to earlier?"

I nodded.

She looked as though she had just had a realization of sorts.

I looked down into my drink, swirling the ice through the pinkish liquid, feeling the cool condensation against my fingers.

"Guilty as charged," I admitted, stepping around any other admission I could tell she was looking for. "Now, Killer Goats aside, why were you hiking the Colorado Trail?"

Remi shrugged again. "It's a long story."

I made a gesture to motion around the room. The rain had started again sometime after lunch and hadn't let up since. "We've got time."

Remi exhaled out of the side of her mouth, making her perfectly coiffed hair move slightly from the burst of air. "Well, okay. I'll give you the Cliff Notes version. I had a friend named Jonah."

I tried to keep my face as blank as possible, not having a clue where the story was going.

"It was a few years ago, right when things started to get really bad between Alison and I." She paused, meeting my eyes for a moment, as if regretting what she had just said. She took a deep breath. "Jonah was really into rock climbing, and he got me into it, too. That was our thing. We'd fly somewhere—"

"Sorry, pause. Did you say *fly* somewhere?" I'm sure my eyes were the size of saucers.

"Yeah," she said, looking confused. "I have my pilot's license, of course."

"Really?" I asked. "I mean, I knew that your father owned an airline, but I didn't realize—"

She cleared her throat. "None of that matters. Anyway. So, we'd fly somewhere to go climb off the beaten path, you know? Places it'd take days to drive to otherwise."

I nodded, feeling properly chastised for interrupting once, afraid to do it again.

"We were climbing, he fell, his leg broke, and we were too far away from the plane for me to get him back."

"Oh my god, did he die?" I couldn't help myself. I held a hand to my chest.

Remi looked surprised, like I should be embarrassed of how dumb my question had been. "No, he didn't die of a broken leg, but he was in bad shape. It took me five hours to get him to the plane. We didn't have a cell signal. I was an idiot and didn't have a satellite phone. I honestly thought he *might* die, to be honest. The bone was," she paused, making a hand motion that I couldn't interpret, then waved her hand in the air as though to dismiss it. "Anyway, it was fucking awful. The surgery didn't go well, there was an infection—they ended up having to amputate it. That's how bad it got."

"Whoa," I whispered, shocked.

"The stubborn bastard wouldn't just let me pay for his surgery. He was making good money, of course, but he couldn't work while he was injured, and he had kids and a wife... I just felt so helpless about it. So, I made up this fundraiser about hiking the Colorado Trail in his honor and have people sponsor me, then I'd use all the money from that to pay for his medical bills. I thought if it was a little more public, he'd have no choice but to accept the funds."

She shrugged, draining her drink.

Wow, that was one of the most absurdly selfless and stubborn things I'd ever heard. It felt a lot like a Remi thing to do, tying good deeds up in complications.

"Did you do it? Did you hike the trail and pay for his bills?"

She nodded. "Sure did."

"People really sponsored you to do that?" I was impressed.

She laughed. "Kind of. It was mostly my own money, but he didn't have to know that."

"Wow, you're a regular Mother Theresa," I joked, not knowing what else to say. If I gave her any real praise, her head might swell too much and she'd never be able to get her sweater off.

Remi rolled her eyes. "They've wanted to Canonize me for years, but you know, the public appearances would really take a toll on my work schedule."

I narrowed my eyes. "So, what is it that you actually do?"

She smirked. "I'm VP of an airline."

I nearly spit out my drink. "Casual." I thought she bought this place with trust fund money. "Your father's?"

She nodded slowly, her expression hardening.

"But VP is impressive for a person so young."

She nodded again, and I could see the muscles in her jaw working. I'd hit a nerve somehow.

"How does one actually run an airline?" I asked, trying to slightly alter the subject as I leaned back into the couch cushions and finished my own drink.

She took my glass and got up, pulling bottles out of the cupboards as she recreated the cocktails. As she sliced a lime open, she said, "Well, I'd be lying if I didn't admit it does help to have a family history. After MIT—"

"So, you ended up going to MIT after all?" I asked, my hand balling into an involuntary fist in the fabric of the throw blanket.

She nodded, her blonde hair falling over her forehead. She pushed it back with her forearm, the fabric of her shirt tightening around her shoulder and bicep. Not that I noticed.

I had a million questions. Was Boston all she wanted it to be? Was she happy there, living the life she had promised me with another woman?

Stormy raised her head and sneezed loudly, startling me.

"Bless you," I said to her, and she wagged her tail lazily in response. She yawned and stretched, climbing down from the couch to walk to the back door. "I think she wants to go outside." I was so grateful for the break in rising tension.

"Oh, let me get her leash," Remi said. After the accident, we'd fashioned paracord into a slip lead of sorts, afraid she'd run away or slip down an eroding hill again.

"I can take her," I said, wanting the fresh air and space.

Remi narrowed her eyes slightly, clearly picking up on my terse tone. "Okay. But, be careful. There's bears and mountain lions, so, if you hear something, come back."

"Bears?" I glanced out the window suspiciously.

"And mountain lions." She nodded with a solemn face. "Just stick close to the house and you'll be okay."

"Why? Bears understand trespass laws?" My voice was slightly squeakier than I appreciated.

"Do you want me to come with?" She asked.

I looked out the window, trying to envision pulling Stormy away from a bear. "Uh..." I shifted my weight and Stormy whined, pulling slightly towards the glass door.

"How about I stand on the porch to oversee, and you can take Stormy down the stairs to pee or whatever," she said.

I nodded, walking outside with Stormy and Remington. Remi paused at the top of the stairs, leaning on the railing, covered from the rain that still drizzled from the sky.

I shivered as I walked down the stairs. The rain had definitely cooled down the August night. I tried to keep close to the house and under cover, but still give Stormy enough smells to encourage her to hurry it up.

I turned back, seeing Remi standing on the second story deck, silhouetted against the house as she watched me. She held a drink in her relaxed hand, and her posture was casual. I was marooned at a house with a stranger who I had once known better than my own self, but now I don't know if I'd recognize her blindfolded. She was different—colder, scarred, and yet still stupidly charismatic when she wanted to be.

The rain made the air thick and musky, mixing with the trees and dirt and the freshest air I'd ever smelled. Stormy snorted as she sniffed the ground, daintily walking around larger puddles.

It felt so typical, so familiar somehow. I looked back over my shoulder at Remi. What was it about her that made me feel like a hurricane? My emotions were being spun so quickly, I wasn't sure which way was up anymore.

I had missed her so much.

And I hated her for that.

Even so, I felt some strange, strong pull to her, which was absurd. She was not my soulmate. She was just an unfairly attractive, extremely charming, confident, funny person. A person who could offer me $100k without a second thought. Did I really want that kind of impulsiveness around? Absolutely not.

Stormy squatted, finally finding a spot worthy, and I heard a twig snap near me, a rustle of leaves. Stormy didn't seem to notice, but the hair on the back of my neck stood straight up. Was it a bear? Was it a mountain lion? Was it a ghost?

I gasped, looking around quickly. I heard nothing else over the rain. The darkness beyond the lights of the house was so vast—made all the more terrifying by the quiet.

The second that Stormy finished, I turned on my heel and raced back up the stairs as fast as I could.

"What's wrong?" Remi looked alarmed, reaching out to me but dropping her hand instead of taking my shoulder.

"I heard something," I said, panting. Stormy let her tongue loll, smiling and wagging her tail after the excitement of a stair sprint.

Remi looked into the darkness behind me. "I don't see anything, but I have a camera on that edge of the house." She grabbed her phone from her pocket.

I turned, afraid to have my back to the boundless, completely black open area. My heart raced. I had definitely heard something.

Her brow furrowed as she concentrated down at her phone. Then, her eyes widened and her face split into a grin. "Well, there's definitely something," she said, clearly trying to stifle a laugh.

"What? What is it?" I moved beside her, desperately squinting at the phone.

There, mere feet from where I had been standing, was a raccoon waddling along the side of the house.

"It's probably rabid," I said quickly to cover my embarrassment.

"Tell you what. You never bring up those Killer Goats again, and I'll never bring up this Rabid Raccoon, either." Remi held out a hand to shake.

I nodded, shaking her hand in strange understanding. I watched the corner of her mouth quirk up in a grin.

We walked back inside, using a towel to wipe off Stormy's muddy feet. She pushed her ears back in a pitiful look as we did it, but the guilt was easier to withstand than muddy paw prints throughout the house.

I kicked off my shoes and walked back to the couch. "You know, I know we can't talk about Goats-That-Must-Not-Be-Named, but do you remember the night you convinced me to streak in the blizzard?"

Remi raised one eyebrow, grabbing the cocktails off the counter and walking back to join me on the couch. "Ah, the night Mack lost a toe to frostbite." She handed me a glass and made painfully obvious eye contact with me as she sipped her drink.

My cheeks flushed. "Really? That's where your mind goes? Not you falling into the snow drift because you couldn't feel your legs? And then security chasing us, and I basically had to carry you?"

"Didn't Cameron initiate this?" Remi rolled her eyes. "That's what you get for listening to Cameron."

"Okay, a good point, but remember you had the silly idea that we should climb to the roof of the Student Union building?"

"An excellent idea." Her tone was confident and nodded with emphasis.

"For a person that could feel their legs."

"I was doing fine on the ladder until you freaked out."

"Yeah, if 'fine' was you slipping and using me to brace

your fall." I was already laughing at the memory. Remi yelling, panicking that she'd hurt me as she'd landed on top of me. "And that's why you don't drink large amounts of beverages mixed in garbage cans."

She grinned. "Look, pin this on me all you want, but I wasn't the one who took one look at my bloody lip and started screaming, making security come after us *again*. Some pre-med student you were."

"So much blood," I countered. "You lost a literal tooth, my friend."

"I got it fixed." She pointed to the incisor that had been missing for a month or two after the Frostbite In Places That Should Not Be Named escapade. "Would have been an excellent view, though."

"Yeah, watching your ass land on my face was a terrible view." I laughed even harder.

"I clearly beg to differ." She tried her best to look serious, but her mouth cracked back into a smile.

She was smiling, but not laughing as hard as I was. Maybe the mental image of a young Remi flying through the air naked, yelling that she couldn't feel her legs made it that much funnier.

"You're missing a vital part of this story." She sipped her drink while watching me over the rim.

I shook my head quickly, my mouth drying at the realization. "No, I think that's the gist of it."

"Remember how you warmed me back up after the bleeding stopped?" Her eye contact turned intense.

I shook my head again. No, we were not going there. I cleared my throat, taking a drink, letting the fruity liquid slide over my tongue.

"I think I distinctly remember something about your face being a major part of it, except we had gotten into that private bathroom near the gym. The one with the shower and the chaise."

I glared at her. "I don't remember." I knew she was crossing the line. So then, why was heat blooming between my legs at the thought? The mood in the room had turned tense. I could hear nothing but the fire pop and crackle, my own breathing coming a bit faster now.

"But, you know, memory is a funny thing." She took a deep breath and lifted a shoulder in a shrug, her forced nonchalance doing nothing to deflate the tension.

"It's late. I should go to bed," I said, walking into the kitchen to set my glass in the sink.

She looked up at me, her eyes intense. It was so plainly written on her face—she wanted me.

Back in college, I remember lying awake, watching her sleep, and wondering why she had chosen me. Why this charming, attractive, goddess of a woman would choose *me*.

But, I suppose, in the end, she hadn't truly chosen me.

I wasn't a young girl who needed Remi riding up on a white horse, ready to sweep me off my feet. I was a woman, and I'd been alone for a long time.

Our chemistry was the one thing I'd never questioned when I tried to piece apart what was real and what wasn't. Remi had been the cartographer of my body, like she knew it better than even I did. Knew every freckle, every dimple. There was a specific kind of seduction in that level of knowing, in the vulnerability of letting someone map your body, explore, journey.

As she followed me into the kitchen, setting her own glass on the counter near the sink, I paused. She looked down at me, a question in her eyes that made my entire body hum in answer.

"It's a pity you don't remember, because I can recall those moments so well," she whispered.

I remembered them, too, in stunning clarity. A clarity that was currently lacking for the moments of heartache in the past decade.

"The sex was never a problem for us, Remi. The problem was the rest of it." I was determined to stay strong even though my entire body longed to melt into hers again.

She shook her head, stopping me from leaving the room by grabbing my wrist. "Then, do we have a problem?"

I longed to scream, *how could we not?* How could fucking her mean nothing after it had once meant everything?

"Not an inspiring pep talk," I said, pulling my wrist from her grasp.

She leaned back on the counter. "You're right. That was an asshole thing to say. I honestly just meant that it doesn't have to mean anything more... just... it is what it is."

"It is what it is?" I asked, watching her. How could I want to scold her for the audacity and want it so badly at the same time? How could I want to run head first into something I knew would be a massive mistake.

It was just the loneliness talking, the memories, the proximity, the stress of the last 36 hours.

She stood. "It's just you and me, Julia."

Just us and the relentless weight of memory.

I closed my eyes as my hands fisted in the fabric of her sweater.

CHAPTER EIGHT

REMINGTON

SURPRISE WASN'T THE RIGHT WORD. COMPLETE bewilderment?

I thought I had crossed the line, and I couldn't stop myself.

The second I had taken her wrist, I was a swirling mixture of need and regret. Why was I so weak around her? Why couldn't I clear my head?

Maybe I just needed to get it out of my system. Maybe I was romanticizing the times we had together. She had hurt me to an extent that I didn't know another human could— so then, why couldn't I keep my hands to myself?

The kiss from the previous night had nothing on this one. Where that kiss was a sloppy, desperate search for an answer, this kiss was a demand. We both knew what we wanted.

We both knew what this was.

Her lips were so soft and tender, and I reached to hold the back of her head in one hand as the other came to her waist, holding her to me. Her arms wove up and around my neck, her grip tight. Her tongue slid across my lower lip, then she gently nipped the same spot.

Something awakened within me at that. Some fire within my belly reignited, and I was consumed by the feeling. The thrill of her, the want of her. I'd never experienced anything like it.

She was unsteady on her tip-toes, clinging to me as I moved to kiss and bite at her earlobe, her jaw, her throat—anything I could get my mouth on.

"This isn't a good idea." She was breathless, her eyes still closed, her hands roaming my back and shoulders as she pressed her hips into mine.

"Of course it isn't," I answered, murmuring across her collarbone as my hand moved to grip the soft roundness of her ass. The leggings I'd given her earlier were tight over her hips, and I'd be lying if I said I hadn't been staring at her for hours, wanting to pull the fabric off with my teeth.

I pushed the immediate question of *what the fuck was I doing?* to the back of my mind as I hooked my hand under the back of her knee, pulling her tighter against me.

She pulled my sweater over my head, her hand clasping the fabric of my sports bra beneath, reaching under the band to palm my breast.

I scooped her up, setting her on the cold granite of the kitchen island counter. She wrapped her legs around my waist, holding me close as I kissed her again, cupping her face in my hands.

"Less clothes," she said against my mouth, and I was inclined to agree.

I pulled her shirt over her head, taking in every stunning inch of her skin. Her breasts were so much better than I remembered, nearly spilling over the top of her bra. I hooked my hands under the waist of the leggings, pulling them over her hips as she kicked them off the rest of the way. The softness of her body paired with the heat in her eyes made my mind clear. No distractions. I wanted her at this moment. It didn't have to mean anything.

"Are you just going to stand there staring at me or are you going to fuck me?" She asked, leaning back on the counter.

Wow. That bossiness was new. Heat coursed through my veins.

I fisted a hand in her hair as I kissed her again. "Greedy," I chastised playfully, giving her a more targeted bite on the soft skin above one of her breasts.

I shoved her legs apart and stepped between them, touching her where she needed it most. It wasn't tender. It wasn't gentle. It wasn't emotional. It was just an urgent need that had to be doused before it incinerated us both.

She gasped, tipping her head back as she closed her eyes.

I pushed two fingers inside of her as my thumb continued circling, over and over, staying just outside of the one spot I knew would make her come. She bucked her hips against me, begging me, urging me to give her relief.

And when I was good and ready, when her flushed skin and desperate moans became too much, verging on the edge of lust and nostalgia, I gave her the pressure she was begging for.

She came hard and fast, as though the climax was slamming into her, forceful and draining. I watched with detached wonder, trying desperately to keep from over-thinking it.

She caught her breath, holding a hand to her chest. She looked up at me, her freckled cheeks flushed as her breasts rose and fell in shaky breaths.

I was overcome with the urge to kiss her, to continue, to drag her to the floor and go for round two.

Maybe she recognized that in me. Maybe she knew that we had to limit things now, or we'd risk going too far, too fast.

"Uh, thanks," she murmured, slipping from the counter. She grabbed her clothes off the floor and put her head down, walking as quickly as she could out of the room.

I LAY IN MY BED, my hand hooked under my head as I stared up at the ceiling.

Did she really just *thank* me for fucking her and walk out of the kitchen naked?

I laughed at the realization that it had actually happened. At my feet, Stormy stirred.

When I'd left the kitchen to go to bed, Stormy had been at my side, walking as though it was an easy, familiar routine. She'd jumped up onto the bed and curled up, staring at me while resting her chin on one of her paws.

Wow, the dog wanted to be near me more than the woman I'd just made cry out in pleasure.

I turned onto my side, turning off the nightstand light with a small huff. I shouldn't be upset. My rational mind reminded me that this was exactly what I wanted. I wanted to fuck Julia. I wanted her to return the pleasure. And yet, it shocked me just how much watching her walk out of the kitchen as though nothing had happened made me question whether that was right or not.

It was probably just my damn ego, always getting in the way.

We absolutely shouldn't have done that, but it was fun. It was a one time thing. And now it was out of my system and I didn't need to think about it anymore.

I shifted again and Stormy sighed at the movement.

"Okay, fine, I'll go to sleep," I said aloud to her.

But first, I lifted my phone and sent a quick text to Kelly. "Don't answer this because it's late, but remind me that I need you to scan in a few old files and documents from the office for me."

I silenced the device and tossed it onto the nightstand, frustrated and unsatisfied.

———————

"IT'S LIKE, really muddy. Like way muddier than I'd have thought," Julia said, holding out her arms for balance. She was wearing my muck boots, another tight pair of yoga pants, and one of my looser sweaters, which strained across her breasts. I stifled a smile at the sight.

"What did you expect? It just rained for two days. You're lucky we can be outside at all." I picked my way around a puddle, pausing to give Stormy room to wind her way on the same path. I had her leash tied around my waist.

It was about a mile to my nearest neighbor, an eccentric widow I'd only met once. Darcy? Marcy? Something like that. I'd only seen her once, walking up the path holding a giant bag of what was a truly inexplicable amount of lemons. I'd stopped to offer her help or a ride, and she just laughed at me, shooing me away.

Maybe she was Stormy's owner? It made the most sense, given the proximity. I assumed she'd lived in the area longer than me, and if Stormy wasn't her dog, maybe she knew who she belonged to.

Julia slipped but caught herself, wildly flapping her arms.

"Careful," I said reflexively.

"Oh, you think I should be more careful? The wild and

reckless route has been really working for me so far, though," she said with a laugh.

I resisted the urge to slap her ass for the snarky remark.

"Do you think we'll be able to make it all the way into town? It was a super long drive," she said.

With the bridge being washed out, my Jeep would never make it over the river, so we were taking the scenic route.

"Maybe your neighbor can give us a ride into town so I can figure out a tow truck."

"Maybe." I frowned noncommittally. I wasn't hating the fact that Julia was stuck at my house, but I didn't want to cross into Annie Wilkes territory.

The forest was silent save for our footsteps and breathing and Stormy's snorts of interest whenever we passed a particularly good looking aspen. There were a few bird calls, but nothing too distracting.

A tiny chipmunk ran in front of Julia's feet, its long, fluffy tail sticking straight into the air, and she paused, squealing in what sounded like equal-parts startlement and delight. I couldn't help but laugh as she held her fists to her mouth, watching where it had run with wide eyes.

Stormy barely registered the chipmunk before it had jumped into another bush to hide. Okay, so she wasn't a hunting dog.

"Why do you live so far out in the middle of nowhere?"

"Hear that?"

She paused, listening. "No?" She looked over her shoulder at me.

"Yeah, exactly. No one around. No one bothering me."

"Since when do you hate people? You were like Miss Popular back at school." She fell into step beside me, and I could see she was looking up at me out of her peripheral vision.

I shook my head. "I guess a lot has changed since then," I said. I didn't want to talk about it.

"Is it because Alison cheated on you?" She sounded sincerely curious, not taunting.

Still, the question rubbed me the wrong way. I narrowed my eyes, not looking at her. Who did she think she was, asking such a personal question?

"It's fine, heartbreak does we—"

"I'm *not* heartbroken," I interrupted, correcting her.

Julia snorted. "Yeah, you really seem totally fine, buddy. Just living some kind of Walden life out here."

"It's okay to want to be alone sometimes."

"But it's just so different than who you used to be." She sounded frustrated.

"It's okay to be different than who you were ten years ago," I countered.

Julia paused and I could feel her glare at the back of my head. "I mean, I do sincerely hope you're different than ten years ago," she said quietly, but it echoed around me as though she had screamed it.

"What's that supposed to mean?" I paused, turning back to her.

Stormy barked, and I glanced down at her before Julia took a step to me.

"Oh, I'll tell you what I mean. I mean that you were a fucking asshole ten years ago." Julia glared at me with the same intensity I'd seen the other day when she'd thrown a tantrum in my arms after nearly dying.

"Me? *I* was the asshole?" I asked, laughing in disbelief.

Stormy barked again, and I noticed her hackles were raised.

Julia put her hands on her hips. "Yeah, and a liar."

"Lover's quarrel?" A voice said calmly behind me.

Julia yelped and I jumped, blocking her with my body as I turned around to see Darcy-Marcy standing behind me with her arms crossed. She looked bemused, smirking with her arms crossed over her chest.

I let out a deep breath. "Oh my god, you scared me." I paused, trying to calm my pounding heart.

Julia gripped my arm from behind.

"So sorry to trespass like this. I live up at Peak 8 Ranch, and my bridge went out with the storm, and I was hoping you were home," I explained.

The woman nodded, and I noticed she was wearing a fur hunting hat, a sleeveless shirt, and baggy wool men's trousers. She looked straight out of Grey Gardens.

"Van der Meer, right? You're the plane gal." She held out a hand. "Flossie."

I had been close enough.

"Remington," I said, shaking her hand. At least she wouldn't tell me it was an unusual name, I supposed.

Flossie glanced over my shoulder at Julia, who still had a death grip on my bicep, then down at the dog.

"We found her out in the storm yesterday. Is she yours?" God, had that only been yesterday? I felt like it had been three months ago.

Flossie shook her head. "Not mine. Cute, though."

We stood in an awkward silence.

"Well, I guess you're probably waiting for me to invite you in," Flossie said, her expression blank.

"Oh, I didn't want to presume," I started, trying to be polite.

"Alright then," Flossie turned on her heel and started back up the hill.

"I can't tell if we go with her," Julia breathed into my ear. I'd be lying if I didn't confess her warm breath made tingles run down my spine and goosebumps rise on my arm. No, that was probably just the breeze.

Flossie turned and furrowed her brow. "You coming?"

We climbed the slope up to the woman's house, which was on a similar overlook to mine, but slightly smaller. It looked older, too. More rustic. It blended so well with the trees, you might have missed it if you didn't know exactly what you were looking for.

We walked inside and took off our boots. I hooked Stormy's leash onto the banister of the foyer. "Stay here, okay?" She looked back up at me, wagging her tail with her ears pinned back with uncertainty.

Julia scratched Stormy's ears and gave her a kiss on the slight indent between her eyes. "Don't worry. We'll be back, baby."

Ugh, why was she so endearing mere moments after being the most annoying woman on the planet?

"Y'all want some coffee?" Flossie asked from down the hall.

"Would love some," Julia said politely.

"I'm okay, thank you," I said, unsure just how comfortable I wanted to get in some strange woman's house.

"Oh wow," Julia breathed, looking around. The house was packed with furniture and decor. The woman had never met a wallpaper she didn't love. I counted four separate patterns along the hall to the kitchen.

The house was even more closed off than mine, which felt a bit stifling. We walked into the kitchen, which was tastefully decorated with slightly older appliances, but didn't look outdated by any means.

Julia's eyes were saucers, looking around the room. "I love your style," she said, sounding breathless with awe.

"Thank you," Flossie said. "It's called 'getting to do whatever I damn well please.'"

Julia smiled, raising her offered coffee cup up in a small cheers. "The dream."

Flossie grinned.

"This is going to sound forward, but I don't suppose you're an iPhone person with an extra charger lying around. I misplaced mine." Julia's cheeks darkened, as though she was embarrassed to ask.

Flossie smiled. "I don't have a phone."

I watched Julia's shoulders slump in disappointment.

Flossie continued, "But I do have an iPad. My daughter insisted I try it for books, because you can make the font size as large as you want, did you know that?"

Julia grinned, nodding. "Yeah, I love that. Can I borrow your iPad charger by any chance? Just for even ten minutes."

Did Julia really bring her dead iPhone on this journey in the hope that she'd be able to charge it somewhere along the way? The woman was shameless.

"It's around here somewhere, bébé," Flossie said, opening drawers packed to the brim with random assortments. Playing cards and butter knives in one drawer. Another was entirely filled with sandwich bags packed with the "TY" tags from Beanie Babies.

"How long have you lived here?" Julia asked, sipping her coffee.

"Fifty-five years." Flossie was glowing.

I didn't know what to say.

"You look surprised by that," Flossie said, pointing to me.

"Oh, no. Just impressed, I guess. I don't blame you, though. It's a beautiful spot."

"Yeah, the neighborhood has gone to hell with all these tech millionaires, though." Flossie was still sweeping her hand through drawers. Between a stuffed felt pickle toy and a scrunchie à la 1984, she found the charger in question. She held it up with a look of incredible achievement on her face.

"Nicely done," Julia said with a wide smile.

I shoved my hands in my pockets.

"Oh wait, you're one of those tech millionaires, aren't you, dearie?" Flossie looked at me with an expression that was in no way concerned for my feelings.

Wow, was she colluding with Julia or what?

Julia grinned into her cup as she plugged in her phone. She looked to be having a wonderful time.

"Not tech, no," I said quickly, waving my hand.

"She's the VP of Express Airways," Julia said, looking between us. Was it just me, or did the way she say that make it sound like she was impressed? *Was* she impressed?

"Aren't you a little young to be some airline bigwig?" Flossie put a hand on her hip as though scolding me.

"I've worked hard and gotten lucky along the way." Wow, that was a Forbes magazine quote if I'd ever heard one. I tried not to grimace at myself.

"Sure, kid," Flossie said.

"This Hollywood Regency decadence is just too wonderful. Where do you get your ideas? I love these velvet barstools."

"Pinterest." Flossie sucked air through her teeth, looking down at the chairs.

"Well, you have a good eye." Julia nodded, touching the fabric of the chair.

Flossie smirked. "Thanks. I just like what I like."

Julia giggled. She looked happier with this wacky woman than she had in the past two days with me.

"I'm going to go check on Stormy," I mumbled and shuffled out of the room awkwardly.

Stormy was lying on the rug, her jowls stretched over her two front paws. She lifted her head when I walked in, wagging her tail. At least someone was glad I was around.

I sat on the top step of the staircase, petting Stormy's head. Why were we even here? I heard Julia's loud laugh. At least *she* was having the time of her life.

I looked around the foyer, decked out in various bright shades, packed with plants and textures. And that was just the one room. It made me feel claustrophobic. Did Julia actually like this shit? I'd have to have a talk with her about how there would be none of this pattern on pattern nonsense in my place.

This felt like a cautionary tale for spending too much time alone. Really fucked with the senses, apparently.

Julia skipped into the room, smiling. "Flossie is going to drive me into town. I'll come meet you back at the house after?"

"How will you get back to the house?" I asked, standing. I felt defensive, protective, something else I dared not name.

"I'll figure it out, don't worry," Julia said, rolling her eyes.

"Just don't be walking through the woods at night," I said, my chest clenching at the thought.

"Okay, chill," she said. "I'll be fine."

Flossie walked into the room—she'd traded her fur cap for a cowboy hat.

"Drive safe. Please don't hesitate to call me." I said.

"Okay, Dad," Flossie said, mirroring the annoyed expression of Julia.

I furrowed my brow, frowning. Wow, never knew my hatred for an old lady could be so immediate.

I turned to Julia. "You have my number, right?"

Julia shook her head. "Nope."

"Then, how were you going to call me?"

"Is she always such a square?" Flossie asked Julia in a stage whisper.

"She's just worried because I had some car trouble, that's all." Julia sighed.

"I'm right here," I reminded them.

"Here, give me your phone and I'll put my number in."

This woman, who I saved from certain death not 48 hours before, was now giving me attitude in front of her new friend like a mean middle schooler.

"There. All set." Julia handed me back my phone. She took out her own phone and made me say my number, typing it in diligently before looking up at me expectantly.

"Home before dark."

Julia nodded.

The two new besties walked me outside, and Julia bent to give Stormy a kiss before climbing into the woman's old pickup truck.

I glanced at the license plate, memorizing the numbers, just in case I had to call in a missing person in a few hours.

Stormy and I stood on the side of the road and watched them drive off, maneuvering around a mudslide before curving out of sight.

"I hate this," I said to Stormy. She shifted her weight between her front paws, watching the truck just as diligently as I had.

I glanced up the road, leading to my house, and then down again, leading to my next nearest neighbor. Should I try to see if they knew Stormy's owner? Nah, I'd had enough human interaction to last me for a few more days. I turned to head up the road home.

I sat on the deck, a seltzer in hand, watching the sunset over the valley below. Without the clouds, you could see for miles. My back porch faced a National Forest, which meant deep green conifers as far as the eye could see, then to the right of that peak, the slopes of the Breckenridge Ski Resort. It was stunning even in bad weather, but with the sun glowing off the mountains, it was truly a sight to behold.

Julia had texted earlier to say she was grabbing dinner with Flossie and would be back slightly later than anticipated. What did that mean? And what did it mean that it frustrated me beyond belief?

I wished Julia was there with me. The peculiar ache in my chest at the having her and then the not having her was doing weird things to my brain.

Sex was funny that way—only a momentary thing, over within an hour, maybe two or three if you were very lucky, but it consumed my mind for so long after. My grip on the seltzer can tightened as I recalled her body, bared before me, writhing on the counter under my touch.

I shook my head, trying to physically clear my thoughts. No, I did not have her. There was no *having* Julia. That was not something I wanted.

And yet, I still mourned for the loss of her. For the loss of us, all those years ago. What could have happened if I had never seen those pictures?

As if on cue, Kelly's name popped up on my caller ID.

I took a deep breath and picked up the phone.

"Okay, they're all scanned, and I just emailed them to you," she said. I loved it when she was no nonsense.

"That was fast," I said, flipping my wrist to check my watch. I'd only requested them a half hour ago. She must have been bored at work today.

"Well, I live to serve," she said, her voice dripping with

sarcasm, but I could also hear a bit of a teasing grin behind it.

"What do you think I should do?" I asked, recalling the strange call I'd gotten earlier that day.

"About Guardian?" She asked.

I'd already filled her in on the details, but I trusted Kelly. She'd been my assistant for years, and she never fed me bullshit. I wanted her opinion.

So, when our biggest competitors called me earlier that day, asking me to meet to discuss a possible C-level position, she was the first one I called.

"To be honest, I don't hate the idea," she said. I heard her navigation aim her down Grand Avenue, which was all the way across town from the office.

"You'd tell me if you did think it was a bad idea, right?" I asked, feeling wary about the whole mess. It had been such a fantastic idea a week ago, but now with the complications... And with other complications here... I was beginning to question myself.

"But you never question yourself," Kelly said.

Again with the mind-reading.

"And stop biting your nails," she added.

I paused, realizing that I was, indeed, chewing on my thumb nail.

"What's wrong?" Her voice softened slightly.

"I'm just kind of reconsidering the timing," I confessed. "I don't think it's the right time to leave Express."

"With all due respect, VDM, Guardian is 90% more likely to get Osprey. Isn't that your main goal? Expansion?"

My main goal was to make my father realize who was actually in charge, who was actually running the show when he was off doing who-knows-what. Or who.

"Interesting then, that you're so driven about this while you are also out of town."

"Ha ha," I said, knowing she was right but hating that she knew me so well nonetheless.

"Whatever you say." She was using the voice that she reserved for when I was very drunk or angry beyond reason. It reminded me of the way you spoke to toddlers.

The phone beeped, signalling an incoming call. My heart leapt into my throat, thinking it was Julia. Was something wrong? I pulled the phone away from my ear, checking the ID. I was disappointed to see it was just Mom, then felt guilty. I'd missed three calls from her during the day, but I'd been a little bit busy and in my head about the recruiter.

"Have fun talking to Mrs. Van der Meer. Let me know if you need anything," she said. "Short of coming to Colorado. I just don't do well in the snow."

I grinned.

"And I know it's August, but I don't believe you that Colorado is ever not snowing."

I made a mental note to send her a picture of my view.

"Wait, one more quick favor," I said, explaining one more tiny detail of what I needed.

I hung up with Kelly and called my mother back.

"Hello, mother," I said, sitting up straighter even though I knew she couldn't see me. Some habits were ingrained a little too well.

"Hey darlin'," she drawled in her charming Southern accent. "How's the mountains treating you? Getting all the fresh air you need?"

"Yep. Lots of fresh air." My eyes scanned the tree line at the edge of my property, expecting Julia to burst forth at any moment. Hoping she would, dreading the moment she did. "Did you want to talk about that bomb you dropped yesterday?"

"Well, I know you're very busy, so I don't want to be taking up too much of your time, but I think this would be a better conversation in person. What are your plans for Thursday at around 8am?"

I frowned, considering the implications. Thursday was two days away. "Most likely drinking coffee and working? Why do you ask?"

"Perfect. It just so happens that I'll be arriving at DIA at 7am, and I'll need a lift."

I stood, panic rising within me.

"What do you mean?"

"I don't think I was unclear, honey," she countered. "I'm coming to visit."

I loved my mother, I really did, but that was absolutely the last thing I needed at the moment.

"I can arrange transportation. I'm not sure what condition the Breck airport is in, so it might be safer to just—"

"I already contacted the Breckenridge airport. They said their runways are perfect. And you know I don't trust any pilot but you."

I grimaced. "I'm having the house redone, so it's a little crowded."

"I can stay in town at a hotel, honey. I just want to make sure we understand each other about this, and I know it will be so much easier in person. Don't you agree?"

I scratched the back of my neck, raking a hand through my hair. Maybe compliance was the easiest way forward. "Sure, Mother. I'll arrange it."

"I can't wait to see you." She sounded sincerely excited, but a pit of dread was growing in my stomach. She promised to send me her itinerary and ended the call.

With my mother here, it'd be much harder to explain Julia's presence. Maybe my mother wouldn't recognize her? How was I going to explain all of this?

Even despite all of the chaos, all I wanted was to know Julia would be back safe. I watched the sun lower in the sky, almost completely dipping out of sight behind the Breckenridge resort.

CHAPTER NINE

JULIA

"Okay, you can make it the rest of the way, dearie."
Flossie said as she gave me a hug.

We'd had such a good day in town together. Any other company felt like a breath of fresh air after being cloistered in with Remi, and especially after our fight that morning. Clearly, there was still a lot to talk about, and even more after last night's kitchen excitement.

I'd spent the day scouring every antique and thrift shop within the town limits, but I was disappointed to find that the road was closed between Breckenridge and Frisco, the next town over that the internet had promised me was a treasure trove of thrift and antique shops.

I'd given in and picked up a major piece of furniture without Remi's approval. It was a bed for her master bedroom, but we could easily put it in one of the other four thousand bedrooms in the house if she decided it wasn't for her. Right now, it fit in at Flossie's home way better than it did at Remi's. But I'd shown Flossie all of my tricks with paint stripper and we'd lost track of time playing around with removing the bright pink paint. I just knew it was going to be a beautiful piece.

It was obvious to me that Remi wanted the opposite of Flossie's home decor style, but I couldn't help that I loved it. I was absolutely a maximalist at heart. Flossie had even let me take photos of her place after we'd returned from town. I'd also picked up some small paint jars, a phone charger, new underwear, and a few home decor magazines. If the internet was going to be shoddy up at Remi's ranch, I might as well go a bit analog, flipping through the pages with Rem.

She'd been such a jerk earlier that I didn't know how returning to her home would be. I'd lingered with Flossie as long as I possibly could, but the sun was lowering and I sure as hell didn't want to be picking my way across the land after it fell too dark.

Flossie had given me a flashlight and pepper spray, telling me exactly where to walk. She'd even walked part of the way with me, pointing in the direction of Remi's home.

Was the pepper spray for mountain lions or murders? I'd forgotten to ask as I stuffed it in the canvas tote containing my new purchases.

I couldn't believe I was even entertaining the idea of walking back through the trees, but there was no other choice. The bridge onto Remi's property was still knocked out, and we didn't know when that would be fixed. All of the conifers and aspen looked the same. When was the last time I'd been hiking? Probably up Quandary Peak with the killer goats and a very hungover girlfriend.

I flicked on my flashlight, stubbornly giving into the idea that it was officially too dark in the forest to make my way without it. It was so eerily quiet and still. All I could hear was my own breathing and the gentle rush of pine needles and leaves on my sweater, the squish of damp mud beneath my boots. Despite my dislike for the creepy silence, the woods smelled deliciously fresh. I wanted to bottle the scent and put it in my bedroom back home. It was so calming after a decidedly uncalm few days.

I walked for ten minutes before pausing, turning to the left and right. Was I even heading in the right direction? I knew that Remi's home was slightly up the hill from Flossie's, so surely if I just went uphill, I'd find it eventually, right? How many mansions could be hiding in the woods, after all.

Had we taken such a long time walking to Flossie's in the first place? I glanced over my shoulder, half-expecting the woman to be standing there in her felt cowboy hat.

No, I was alone.

I took my phone out of my bag, cradling it like a precious object in my hand. I'd never take it for granted again. Ever ever. I unlocked it and pressed the call button beside Remi's name. No ring. Nothing. I glanced back down at the screen to find that I had no service.

I looked up at the sky, seeing that the lighter edge was to my right. Okay, that meant West was that way. Remi's house was southeast of Flossie's.

Pssh, I didn't need some fancy wilderness training to get through. I'd be fine.

Five minutes later, I passed a tree that I swore I recognized. Hmm, maybe I'd be fine.

I paused, checking for service again.

"Remington," I called out. Maybe she'd hear me? Maybe I was close? "Flossie?" Maybe I was closer to her home, somehow?

No sound greeted me in return. Not even an echo.

This was the worst idea I'd ever had. I should have just stayed the night at Flossie's, like she'd offered. I just didn't want to spend a night away from Remi while I still had the chance. It was a stupid realization, but a realization nonetheless, and I wasn't going to try to figure out the sentiment without a lot of therapy. That'd just be irresponsible. Best to save it for the professional.

I clenched and unclenched my free hand, looking around with my flashlight. How could I have possibly gotten so turned around? I couldn't even tell there was a slope where I was standing. Just mud and muck.

Panic began to rise in my chest. "Remington?" I called again, trying to project my voice in the general direction I thought was her home.

What if I had to stay the night out here? What if I was all alone? Would a bear eat me? Should I climb a tree and sleep à la Katniss in Hunger Games? No, she only stayed up there because she had rope. I'd absolutely fall out of a tree if I tried to pull that shit.

I called for Remington a few more times, trying to calm the thudding pulse in my ears and chest. My breathing was growing tight, and my arms felt tingly.

Oh my god, *this* was the way I died. Not in a flood accident or car crash, but by being eaten by a bear, or bitten in my sleep by a rabid raccoon, or even overrun by a pack of wild chipmunks. Did chipmunks travel in packs? Why was I picturing tiny switchblades in their hands?

I shook my head. I was already losing touch with reality. How did the people on Naked and Afraid pull it off? They found food, right? And shelter?

Could I fashion a cave out of aspen branches and cover it with pine needles for insulation?

A particularly loud cicada startled me and I tensed, looking around me with the flashlight.

"Remi," I called out again. "Oh my god, if you can hear me, please come find me."

I took a deep breath, trying to get my bearings again, but everything looked the same in the dark.

"If you can find me, I promise to never be mean to you again. I'll decorate your house for free. I'll pay *you*." I looked around with my flashlight.

"I'll make dinner every night, and wash the dishes, especially the colander, because I know you hate that most of all for some weird reason. Even though it's the easiest item to wash."

I walked forward, ducking under a low-lying branch.

"If you find me, I'll do anything. *Anything*. I'll wash the damn colander naked."

I sighed. At least the talking was drowning out the deafening silence closing in on me. "Did you hear me? Naked colander washing. And I'll give you like a fifteen minute backrub."

I looked up, noticing the stars were blazing bright above me. Well, at least I'd die in a beautiful spot. The trees blocked most of the view, though. I bet you could see the entire Milky Way from out here.

I heard rustling in the trees and looked around, cowering, but it stopped. Maybe I'd imagined it.

My voice was quivering, and I knew I was on the verge of panic-tears. "Okay, a twenty minute backrub. I mean, hell, I'd go down on you for hours if it meant you'd find me out here," I said, pushing through another branch.

I felt a little scandalous saying it out loud, but hey, maybe the bears would see how serious I was and leave me alone.

A light flashed across my face and I gasped in surprise.

"Jude?" Remington asked, breathless. I couldn't see her past the light, but I'd recognize her voice anywhere.

"Rem," I said, running towards her and the light. Wait,

was I dying? Was I supposed to be running *towards* the light?

Remington lowered her flashlight and looked at me with wide eyes. "What the hell are you doing out here?"

"Just having a little walk," I said, though my voice squeaked with emotion. I bit my trembling lip, feeling relief wash over me at the sight of her.

She barrelled through pine branches and reached for me and pulled me into her. I wrapped my arms around her waist, burying my face in her chest. The hardness of her body, the soft fabric of her sweatshirt, the warmth of her presence.

"I was so worried," she whispered. "You didn't come back, and then I heard you call my name."

"You heard me?" I asked, opening my eyes and feeling my body tense again beneath her arms. Just how much had she heard?

She spoke into my hair, as if holding me tightly wasn't close enough. "I heard two yells of my name and I came barrelling out here. We aren't far from home, don't worry. You okay?"

I tipped my head back to look up at her, though I couldn't see much. "I'm okay. You found me."

"I found you." She sounded as if she was in awe.

Had any uttered sentence ever sounded so bittersweet?

She held me until my shoulders and knees stopped quaking.

"I thought a bear might eat me," I confessed as she pulled away. She took my hand, holding her flashlight like a beacon of strength and navigation in front of us.

"Eat you? Probably not. Maim, perhaps. Leave you for dead and revisit the carcass a few days after? More likely." She laughed as she said it, but I just stared at her in horror.

"You're so mean to me. I'm in a fragile state, you know.

I've been surviving out here for days." I sniffled for added effect and definitely not because tears still welled in my eyes.

"You're right." She squeezed my hand. "Now come on, I've got some dishes for you to wash naked."

I stumbled. "Wh-what?" My entire body flushed. I had no idea my elbows could heat in embarrassment, but here we were.

We broke though the line of trees surrounding the backyard. Stormy stood on the deck overlooking us, silhouetted in the light of the main room. Her tail wagged and she barked in excited greeting.

"That was the deal, right? Or, at least, part of it?" Illuminated in the lights of the house, she turned to me and winked.

"Excuse me, that was a private conversation between me and the Spirit of the Forest." I feigned astonishment to hide my deep shame.

"Really? Because it seemed very... directed." She grinned and held my hand as we walked up the stairs to the back patio.

Stormy bounded over to me, jumping up in excitement. I was grateful for the momentary break in conversation and the excuse to let go of Remi's hand to put some distance between us. I was too happy to be back in her presence for my own good.

Remi leaned on the porch railing. "Wow, not the hero's welcome *I* deserve, Stormy."

I sat down on a lounge chair as I scratched Stormy's chest and chin, catching my breath for the first time since my harrowing and perilous journey. I dropped my bag to the floor.

"I'm sorry you had to come find me," I said quietly. "Thank you, though."

Remi looked at me in silence for a long while. "Any-time." She shrugged, as though she often rescued defense-less women in the woods surrounding her home.

I felt shy and uncertain. I cleared my throat. "Want a drink?"

She nodded, sitting down in the chair next to mine. "Sure. Surprise me."

I walked through the patio door and crossed the main room to the kitchen. My hand slid along the countertop that she had fucked me on the night before. My cheeks flushed again at the memory.

I opened the fridge, looking for beers. None? I sighed. She was really going to make me work for this drink. And after her fancy Paloma-ish drinks and an Old Fashioned I remembered, I wasn't sure I could compete. I straightened, spying the bottle of tequila from the first night. I grabbed two small glasses and carried them out.

"Ah, I see we've gone straight to this," she remarked, one elbow up as her hand was tucked under her head.

I laughed, setting the glasses down on the wooden accent table between our chairs. I poured her a small drink, then filled my own. I handed hers over, then raised mine in a small cheers. "To being out of the woods."

She grinned. "Ah, still into Taylor, I see."

I laughed. "I remain steadfast in my love of Taylor Swift." I sipped the clear liquid, feeling its warmth envelop my tongue, coat my mouth. It didn't need salt or lime. We'd certainly upgraded from the Jose Cuervo we drank at parties in college. I glanced at the bottle, reading the label for the first time. Maestro Dobel? Seemed fancy.

We sat in silence for a long time, listening to the quiet of the night sounds. Cicadas, the wind through the tree leaves, an owl—very faint, but easy to pick out in the otherwise silence.

"I can see why you like living here." I felt peaceful and calm, after my near-death experience.

"Being in Flossie's house has me rethinking hermitage." She said, sighing.

"Why? Because it was packed with... well, everything in the entire world?" I smiled, thinking of the swan wallpaper in the bathroom.

"No, it just seems to have gotten to her, you know? The solitude has made her a bit..."

"Eccentric?" I offered politely.

She nodded. "Sure, eccentric."

I thought of the day with Flossie, how she'd told me about her life as we perused vintage dressers and tables. "I love her. And I think you'll like her eventually, too. You know she used to travel with a circus?"

Remi raised an eyebrow. "As what?"

"I think as a seamstress, but I like the idea of her being a lion tamer, personally."

Remi smiled, her eyes trained on the outstretched darkness before us. "Yeah, that suits her."

"And you'll never guess, but her arms are completely sleeved out in tattoos."

"Seriously?" Remi smirked, sipping her glass. She seemed to be reconsidering her stance on the woman.

We sat in silence for a few more moments.

"I think the stars are the best part," I said, my eyes adjusting to the dark sky.

"They're definitely one of the best parts." She finished her small glass. "Maybe I should buy a telescope."

I nodded. "You really should."

"Alexa, turn off the lights," she said, raising her voice. Nothing happened. "Damn, I forgot the internet isn't working." She murmured.

She stood, setting her glass next to the bottle.

"What are you up to?" I asked, watching her walk back into the house. Stormy followed, and I watched as she hopped up on the couch, curling into a tiny dog donut.

"I want to show you how many stars you can see from right here."

The lights turned off behind me—the darker the house became, the lighter the sky turned. I was amazed, seeing it in such stunning clarity as my eyes continued to adjust to the night.

A familiar riff filled my ears — a steady pluck of a guitar, then a synth keyboard tone. The xx? I turned around to see Remi walking away from the record player at the edge of the room, the familiar song playing out over speakers I hadn't spied on the patio walls. I'd basically had this album on repeat our entire senior year, completely obsessed. It had been the soundtrack to every study session, every drive. and to be honest, quite a few times we were lying in bed for hours.

I hadn't been able to listen to it since.

What was she trying to do here?

She walked back on the patio, tossing a throw blanket on my lap. I gratefully pulled the blanket over my legs and feet, which had grown cold in the evening. I always forgot how cold it turned at elevation, surprised at the intense difference between sunshine and the chill of the night.

"I haven't listened to this in years," I confessed, eyeing her as she sat on the lounge chair near my feet.

"I was so fucking worried when you didn't come back tonight." She looked vulnerable, her expression open and her eyes wide.

"I'm sorry, I—"

She leaned forward and pressed her mouth to mine, her lips soft at first, tentative even in their tenacity.

The same relief that had flooded my body when she'd

found me resurfaced, and I was powerless against it. I kissed her hungrily, starving for her taste, her touch, all of her. I reached to her, pulling her to me until she settled on top of me.

She fisted her hand in the sweater fabric at my waist. "I know this isn't a great idea," she whispered.

I didn't dare respond to that, but in the moment, I truly did not care if it was a good idea or a bad idea. It was all I could think about. It was a consuming idea, shoving away all worries or cares or sensible explanations about why I should absolutely stop. I pushed my hands into her hair, gripping her, clinging to what I could, desperate for her.

My hips pushed into hers, shameless in their quest for friction, for touch, for release.

"I do believe the promise of 'hours' was made," she whispered against my lips, her own smile tightening her lips.

"Oh, is that what you heard?" I joked, pulling her lower lip between my teeth.

I flipped the position, climbing on top of her. She reached up to hold my wild hair out of my face, looking at me with wonder, like she'd never seen me before.

"Well, a promise is a promise," I said, pushing back onto my knees. "Turn around, I'll start your backrub."

She laughed, playfully slapping at my thigh. I reached for her and caught her wrist, my eyes widening in victory. She jerked her arm, changing the grip, and laced her fingers in mine, staring into my eyes as she pulled my finger into her mouth. My entire body tightened as her warm, soft mouth surrounded my finger, sucking gently on my skin.

Was it possible to orgasm immediately from just watching something so incredible? Because I was right on the edge.

She nipped gently at the pad of my finger and I gasped.

"I think you know what I want, and I think you're ready to give it to me."

I'd have given her my left arm at that moment if she'd asked in that voice, my entire body vibrating from the enveloped warmth of her.

I nodded, wetting my lips with my tongue, unable to speak. I reached and unbuttoned her pants, frantic to taste her again.

"Good girl."

I blinked up at her, surprised by how much I liked this side of Remi.

She lifted her hips, helping me as I removed her pants and underwear. I shifted, kneeling on the ground as I took in the bare sight of her while kissing the soft skin of her legs, massaging the hard muscle of her calf and I licked the back of her knee. She sighed in pleasure, her fingers gripping the arms of the lounge chair.

"Fuck, I've wanted this for so long, Julia," she said, winding a hand into my hair. "Please."

I nipped at the soft skin of her inner thigh and she jumped, a grin spreading over her face.

And then my mouth was on her. It was remarkable how memories flooded back at just the taste of her — it was exactly the same as I remembered. It was thrilling and comforting and arousing and heartbreaking all at once. I didn't think it was possible to miss a person so much, so completely, as though a part of me had been missing for the past decade, and I'd just found it.

She had always been the quieter, calmer party during sex — sometimes I didn't know if she was orgasming unless I was watching her expression.

Now, though, she was moaning, pushing her hips into me, calling my name.

I reached up under her sweatshirt, dipping my hand beneath her bra as I found her hard nipple, rolling it between my thumb and forefinger as I devoured her. She held a hand over my own, clutching at me as she cried out in release, her hips lifting from the chair. I wrapped my other arm around her, holding her still, holding her against me as I continued.

As she calmed, gasping for breath, and I lifted my head, seeing her flushed cheeks.

"That wasn't hours, so I owe you a few more of those, I think," I joked, wiping my mouth on her thigh and kissing her warm skin.

She scrubbed a hand over her face. "Fuck, how are you so good at that?"

"This isn't amateur hour, Rem," I joked, settling into the lounge beside her.

I listened to the familiar ending of "Fantasy," how the music faded away, dropping with an electronic pulse. The record stopped. We must have listened to the full side. "I'll flip it," I offered, pushing myself up. "You want some water."

Remi nodded, pulling her dark jeans back over her hips. "Sure, that'd be great."

I walked inside, flipping the record, then grabbed a glass of water to share. When I returned, Remi had shifted so she was sitting up straighter and had poured two more glasses of tequila. Damn, the girl sure knew how to party on a school night.

"You know, tequila always makes me think of that first party," she said, exhaling and staring out over the patio railing.

I sat down on the edge of the lounge before tucking

myself back into the nook under her arm, with my head on her chest.

"You tasted like tequila the first time we kissed." She didn't turn to face me, but I looked up at her, bewildered. One orgasm and she was ready to talk about the good old times? My stomach swirled in a combination of nervous energy and anticipation.

"Well, you'd given me three shots, I suppose that's fair." I rearranged the blanket over us for something to do with my hands.

"Remember when we snuck into the student lounge that night?" She asked, her voice quieter, almost wistful.

"I had lower standards for furniture back then," I joked.

She turned to me, looking completely serious. "Why did you do it?" Her expression became pained.

"Do what? Fuck you on a gross couch in a public place?" I shrugged.

Her eyebrows raised in surprise and she finished her drink in one quick shot. "I've thought about it almost every day for ten years, trying to replay what went wrong. Why you would do that to me, trying to piece it all together."

My body tensed. "What are you talking about?"

"You went back to him. After I asked you to start a life with me." Her brows drew together.

I thought that perhaps I'd lost my mind in the woods earlier that evening, but here she was, talking complete nonsense. "Went back to who?" I tried to remain calm, talking very slowly in order to understand. I pushed myself up to have a better look at her.

"Curtis."

I almost laughed. Curtis was a hippie DJ that I'd dated before Remi, and dated was a loose term. We'd made out at a party a few weeks before the end of the spring semester my Junior year, then visited each other a few times over the summer, but by the first week of fall, we realized we actually had nothing in common. We'd never even had sex. "What in the world are you talking about?"

She pulled up her phone and swiped the screen a few times, then handed it to me. "I know you did, Julia."

I looked down at the screen, seeing a grainy photo of the front of my dorm building. I squinted, realizing I was standing in front of it. Goosebumps raised over my arms as I studied the surveillance photo. "What the fuck is this?"

Remi didn't answer.

"This is some very creepy private investigator shit," I said, remembering the jeans from the photo "Why do you have a photo of me standing in front of the dorm?"

"There's more. You can scroll if you want." She looked away from me, swallowing.

My hands shook as I looked through the photos. There were about ten photos with me, then the photos switched slightly, and there was someone with my clothing and hairstyle — easy enough to accomplish, it'd just been in a pair of french braids. Then another person was in the photos, and the two were kissing, then "I" lead him into the building. I guess if you squinted, it could be Curtis. In fact, I was almost positive that it *was* Curtis.

"Why did you take these?" I asked, my mouth dry with nerves.

"I didn't. I don't know who did. They just showed up in my mailbox one day with no return address. It was a pretty fucked up thing to do." Remi grimaced.

I scrolled further, horrified and curious in the same way I couldn't look away from car crashes on the side of the road. I knew I might see some mangled, awful scene, but I couldn't stop myself.

Phone logs. I zoomed in, seeing my number calling the same number over and over. After the phone logs were supposed text message transcripts, where my number was texting obscenely sexual and graphic things to someone. The last one listed was, "Remi can't find out."

I looked up at Remi in stunned disbelief. "What is this?"

"You tell me." Remi looked hardened, and her tone was robotic.

"You broke up with me because someone badly photoshopped these documents?" I wanted to throw her phone as far as I could, over the railing and down into the valley below.

She blinked. "Of course you say that they're photoshopped. Of course."

Frustration and rage and confusion and a sense of injustice bubbled inside of me, ready to explode.

"How do I know you're not just lying?"

"Why couldn't you have just *asked* me? Or asked Curtis?"

"I did ask Curtis," she exclaimed, her face reddening.

I stood up, nearly unable to breathe. This wasn't happening.

"And you know what he said? He confirmed all of it. All of it." She stood, too, taking the phone out of my hands. Maybe she could read my mind that I was ten seconds from hurling it into the abyss.

"But why didn't you ask me?" My voice cracked and hot, mad tears stung my eyes.

She paused, looking me up and down.

"Don't you think it's a little suspicious?" I asked, my lungs a fist inside of my chest.

She stared down at the phone in her hands.

"I've literally never even said the word cunt! And you know I hate the word panties. And we were *not* on the anal level." I stomped my foot in an overflow of emotion. "Plus, the clothing changes between the pictures of me alone and the pictures of me supposedly with Curtis. Look for yourself."

She held up her phone, staring at the screen as her fingers swiped back and forth.

"You fucking knew me better than that. Why didn't you just ask me?"

"I was so mad. I was going to ask you about it in person when we got back to school. And then you never came back." Her forehead creased, and she quickly wiped tears from her cheeks.

"I never went back because you fucking ruined me," I screamed. "I couldn't get out of bed for months. My aunt thought I was going to kill myself, and she made my cousins watch over me day and night." I walked to the railing, gripping it with white knuckles. "I can't fucking believe you thought that. With Curtis of all people. And then you emailed me the engagement announcement."

Remi paused, looking confused. "What?"

"You emailed me a link to look at the announcement in the Times," I said.

"Hey, that's not," Remi started, walking to the railing. "I didn't do that. I didn't even know we had an announcement."

"Sure, I bet," I said hastily, sniffling.

She took hold of my arm and I wrenched it out of her grasp. She held her hand in midair, her eyes wide. "Why would someone do this to me? To us?"

I wanted to slap her, but I settled for digging my

fingernails into my palms instead. I sniffled again, taking a deep breath. "Who wanted you to marry Alison?"

Remi paused, looking out into the darkness. She sniffled, putting her hands over her face. She burst into heart wrenching sobs, the kind that sounded as though they were ripping you apart as they burst out.

I put a hand on her shoulder and she flinched, moving away.

"I just need some space," she said, turning and disappearing into the house.

I stood in stunned silence, watching her go.

CHAPTER TEN

I AWOKE WITH THE DIM LIGHT OF DAWN SLIPPING PAST THE curtains. I blinked, sitting up. I'd slept in my clothes above the blankets. I hadn't even taken off my shoes. I kicked them off, stretching.

Had the night before been a dream? Or had that really happened? Had I believed a lie for the past ten years, setting my life on a track that I never wanted?

And it had all been my father's fault.

I wanted to curl into a ball and go back to sleep and wake up in another ten years.

What would I even say to her? What *could* I say? I thought my head might explode the night before.

I had never been close with my dad. He treated me like a business colleague since before I could remember. I had always been expected to follow in the family footsteps, and I had. I'd played right into his little game.

Except for two times in my entire life.

First, when I wanted to go to McManus College. McManus was a small college in the mountains of

Colorado, not exactly known for producing millionaires. He'd wanted me to go to Cornell, just like him. But, he'd accept McManus once I showed him my five-year plan of going straight from college to my MBA at MIT. And I'd done exactly that, in the end.

Second, when I'd invited Julia to go with me. But that had been settled quickly enough with his little scheme. I wondered how much he had paid Curtis.

Which was why walking in on him fucking my wife was both a shock and to be expected. I'd surrounded myself with snakes — why was I so surprised that they bit me?

I grabbed my phone, calling Kelly immediately.

"Good morning, Remington," she said politely.

"Hey, Kelly. So, I know I sounded a little strange yesterday questioning Guardian's interest, but now I want to go for it. Full steam ahead." I didn't want anything to do with my father's company.

She paused, clearing her throat.

"What's the matter?" I asked.

"I'm going to have Jones call you." She had switched right back into her overly kind voice.

"Tell me."

"No, ma'am. You don't pay me enough to give you bad news."

"I'll give you a raise," I said quickly, desperate.

"I'll have Jones call. Is there anything else you need?"

I stood, dread growing in my stomach. "Tell me as a friend, not as an assistant. Please."

She paused. I'd never begged her before.

She lowered her voice. "Jones says the Board is ready to make the move to buy Osprey, but the investors are feeling a little jumpy. You've been MIA lately, and they don't know if you can handle this."

Fuck.

"That's not my fault. We lost power. I haven't had internet for three days, Kelly," I said, pacing around the room.

"It's not that. It's from before that. It's the last eight months.."

"My divorce is making me seem unstable?"

I swear I could *hear* Kelly shrug noncommittally.

"That's a double standard. Would they have ever questioned me if I was a man getting a divorce?" I glared at the wall.

"Even though that may be the case, this is the reality."

I raked a hand through my hair. "Thank you for telling me."

"Is there anything else?"

I stared up at the ceiling, biting my lip. "One more thing."

I filled Kelly in on the details of picking up my mother, and she said she'd handle the transportation from DIA to a regional airport where I could pick her up. Kelly was a godsend. I made a mental note to give her a raise. A ten billion dollar bonus should be sufficient, right?

I changed clothes, brushed my teeth, and combed my fingers through my hair to contain the erratic bedhead that had appeared overnight.

I walked down the stairs, both afraid to face Julia and worried she wouldn't be there. I didn't know which prospect seemed worse.

I assumed Stormy had stayed with her for the night, because I'd flaked. Dog guardian guilt welled in my stomach. I couldn't handle anything in my life properly, could I?

This was why I preferred to be alone.

I found Julia sitting at the kitchen island, eating a bowl

of cereal as she flipped through a magazine. Her eyes flicked up to me then back down to the magazine.

Stormy lay on the ground near her feet.

I walked into the kitchen, pouring myself a cup of coffee and paused, looking at her.

The kitchen was silent except for the scrape and clink of her spoon. She had a scoop of peanut butter stuck to the inside edge of her cereal bowl and was picking it up bit by bit to add to each bite. I recalled her doing something similar back in college, thinking it was such a weird habit until I'd tried it. I'd somehow forgotten how delicious it was.

She looked up at me again, chewing slowly. She looked wary, as though I would explode if given the wrong expression.

"About last—" I began.

"Well, last—" She began at the same time.

We both paused.

"No, you go," I said.

She sighed. "You get the space you needed?"

Damn, she wasn't beating around the bush this morning. "Kind of."

She nodded, eating another bite of cereal.

"I'm sorry," I said.

"For which part?" She raised her eyebrows with an exceptional amount of attitude.

I deserved that. I sipped my coffee. "I should have talked to you."

"Yeah, you should have," she said. "I tried calling you so many times. For weeks."

I'd blocked her number in a fit of rage. I scratched the back of my neck. "And I'm sorry for that."

She nodded slowly. "My entire life was upended because of your stubborn stupidity."

I nodded, ashamed.

"And I made the choice to not go back, so that's on me, but you wasted no time in getting engaged."

"We didn't even get engaged until that summer," I said, wrinkling my forehead.

"Jeez, do you never Google yourself? Look at the announcement." She rolled her eyes.

"I'm being honest when I say that there was no announcement in the Times," I said.

She sighed, picking up her phone. She typed something in, taking another giant bite of cereal as she stared at the screen, apparently waiting for something to load. Her cheeks were puffed in the cutest chipmunk impersonation I'd ever seen.

Then, her eyes narrowed. She swallowed, looking up at me. "Did you take it down or what?"

I shook my head, leaning forward as she held the screen up to me to show... nothing? "No, I'm serious. There was no announcement in the Times."

She returned to clicking around on her phone, pulling up her email app. "Here, let me find the stupid link." I watched her type in my name and saw dozens of unreturned emails. I'd blocked her there, too. I was such an impulsive asshole.

She pulled up the email and showed me my own name connected to an email address I didn't recognize. There was nothing in the body of the email, only a link with the URL containing both me and Alison's name.

She clicked on it, and it opened a page with some announcement I'd never seen. I took the phone from her, reading it over. Goddamn, I'd have broken up with me, too, reading this bullshit. The page looked off, though. First, it wasn't optimized for mobile. Second, all of the "recent" articles were around March 2010, as well.

Suspicious, I returned back to the email, looking at the URL. It seemed legit. I opened it again, checking the URL in the browser bar.

"Ah ha, I see what's up here," I said, pointing to the URL. "This directed you to nytime.com. It's nytimes.com, isn't it?"

She pulled the phone back from me, looking at the page with renewed intensity. "Are you fucking kidding me?"

I resisted the urge to rub it in that I wasn't the only one who could be tricked.

"Who did this?" She asked, staring at her phone in disbelief.

"I think I know," I said, sipping my coffee. "My father."

"What did your dad have against us?"

"I don't think it was personal," I said.

She pointed to the phone. "Feels fucking personal."

"No, I mean, I don't think it was about you." I didn't exactly know where to start. "Alison's family has connections, and I think he wanted to use me for that."

She blinked, pushing her cereal bowl away from her. "Then why did you agree to marry her?"

"How much time have you got?" I said, refilling my coffee cup. I held up the carafe as an offer. She reached for her cup and slid it across the counter for me.

"Time is the one thing on our side. Finally," she said with a small nod.

I leaned on my elbows on the counter and explained how Alison and I had known each other since grade school — that part of the story was true — and how after the breakup with Julia, I'd been so heartbroken that I'd accepted that I'd never love anyone again. My father made a deal with me that I'd get my trust as soon as I turned 25, or when I married, whichever came first. Anxious to get financial independence — hilarious considering I knew I'd be joining his company anyway, I chose marriage. And I chose it with a woman that I knew wasn't in it for love, a woman who would have no expectations of the kind of life I'd give her. A woman who could never break my heart.

My mother had been the one to talk me into it, in the end. She'd told me to consider Alison as a business partner. She'd be comfortable, but we'd be a partnership, not a couple. And for years, Alison was fine with it. I think she was glad to appease her parents just as I was, as fucked up as that seemed. She had outside relationships, that wasn't the issue. We were open simply out of necessity.

It was when I walked in on her with my father that the entire facade really came crumbling down.

Talk about traumatizing. Talk about a mental image that I couldn't shake, no matter how hard I tried.

Julia stared at me with wide eyes, her lips slightly parted in shock.

"What does your mother think of that?" She asked in a quiet voice.

"My parents separated right after college. Right after Alison and I got engaged, actually," I said.

"I'm so sorry to hear that," she said.

"No, it's really one of those better off situations. They were miserable together for years. Now they only pretend to be together for the public image aspect."

She nodded solemnly.

"How are your parents? I realize I never asked."

She smiled. "They're good. They live in Wisconsin now."

I grinned. "Wow, who would give up Colorado for Wisconsin?"

"Do you know how cheap it is to live there? They have an old house down the street from Lake Michigan and they pay like 1/3 of what I do in rent in Denver." She laughed, shaking her head.

I nodded. "Still, though. Colorado's pretty perfect."

She looked as though she was biting her tongue. "Sure."

"What?" I asked, though I was pretty sure I knew the answer.

A car horn blared outside, startling me. Stormy lifted her head, woofing in the direction of the front door.

"What the hell is that?" Julia asked, looking towards the front door.

I stood, walking to the front door. I looked out the window towards the driveway. "Well, I'll be damned." It was Flossie, waving at me from her truck.

I opened the door, stepping out onto the porch.

She honked the horn again with a wide smile on her face. "Can Julia come out to play?"

I couldn't help but laugh.

Julia appeared beside me, waving back at Flossie before taking off across the porch to greet her in the driveway.

I grabbed boots from inside the door, telling an excited Stormy to wait inside as she wiggled, trying to get past me.

"I got you a little present," Flossie called out to me past Julia.

"Oh yeah?" I asked, nervous about what that could mean as I walked towards her.

"I called up my friend Ray and he patched your bridge this morning." She looked proud of herself.

"Really?" Julia said, looking down the driveway.

"Well, I didn't get here on my magic carpet," Flossie said, laughing. "It's nothing fancy, just some wooden planks with support, but it'll get you over the gap until you can fix it properly."

"You're an actual goddess," Julia said, reaching to touch Flossie's arm in an affectionate squeeze.

Wow, they really were besties, weren't they? That had been fast.

"Have you eaten yet?" Flossie asked.

"Yeah, but I can always eat more. That has never been my problem," Julia laughed, and I grinned. I'd always been envious of women who were confident in their bodies, and Julia had become the epitome of that. It was incredibly sexy to witness.

"Want to drive on into town and have some proper breakfast?" Flossie asked.

Julia looked back at me. "Can Remi come?"

Flossie rolled her eyes, as though she was really considering it. "I guess," she said. She winked at me, pointing a thumb to the passenger side.

"You don't want to take my Jeep down?" I asked.

"Ugh, these tech millionaires and their Jeeps." Flossie sounded exasperated.

CHAPTER ELEVEN

JULIA

I watched Remi across the booth cut her pancakes into a perfect grid. I was definitely a chaotic pancake eater, digging in wherever I could, not caring if I perfectly aligned all three cakes into each bite.

Flossie sat next to me wearing an oversized long-sleeved linen shirt rolled up to her elbows and loose-fitting jeans. On her thin, elderly frame — I'd guess she was in her early 70s — she looked effortlessly cool. I hoped I had such style when I was her age. Hell, I didn't even have that much style now. My current style was: Which of Alison's pants will fit my curves and which of Remi's shirts will fit over my chest? It was a very fun game each morning.

Maybe I'd have Remi buy me a new blazer, seeing as how she ruined it and all. Fair was fair.

"So, let me get this straight, y'all dated in college," Flossie said, holding her coffee mug with both hands. She had silver bangles on both wrists, accenting the dark ink visible on her forearms.

Remi nodded, looking warily at me, then back to Flossie.

"And then you," Flossie pointed at Remi. "Broke this angel's heart."

Remi took a deep breath. "Well, not exactly—"

"Yeah, that's the gist of it," I said with a smirk.

Flossie looked back to Remi with raised eyebrows. "How are you not grovelling for forgiveness right now? Have you *met* her?" Flossie turned to me with a gesture akin to Vanna White holding a fork and knife covered in maple syrup.

I grinned.

Remi laughed, shaking her head.

"Listen, if I were forty years younger, Julia." She smirked, elbowing me in the side.

"I fully intend to make it up to her, I promise," Remi said, wiping her mouth on her napkin.

Why did my stomach leap at that comment?

Or was it the way Remi was looking up at me through her lashes, a little shy.

I cleared my throat, fidgeting by pouring more coffee from the carafe into my mug. Remi held hers out for a top up, too.

"I don't think I realized how bad the damage was in town," Remi said, changing the subject.

I'd noticed the day before, but Remi seemed more and more upset with each downed tree, closed street, and flooded home that she saw.

"Yeah, it's awful," Flossie said. "I've given a boatload of money to the local mutual aid."

"Oh, that's awesome," I said, feeling strangely proud of my new friend.

Remi nodded, looking thoughtful.

"Well, shall we show Remington what we found yesterday?" Flossie asked.

I grinned.

"Wait, what am I getting signed up for?" Remi's expression showed alarm, looking back and forth between the two of us.

"The grovelling sure needs work," Flossie sighed, climbing out of the booth beside me.

I quickly chugged my coffee, regretting the decision to pour scalding hot liquid down my throat at warp speed, and took a sip of ice water before climbing out after her.

Remi made a motion for me to take the lead as she fell into step beside me.

We walked through the small diner and exited onto the street. Flossie had chosen a place off of the main thorough-fare, and instead the spot was packed with local charm — none of the tourist nonsense I'd always found in Breck before.

"I have to talk to you about something," Remi started.

I turned my head, all ears.

"My mother is coming tomorrow," she said. She rubbed at the back of her neck as we followed Flossie down the street.

"What? How?" I asked. The road from the interstate into town was still closed.

"I'm flying out to Denver to pick her up."

I paused. "Do you think I could come with you?"

"Come with me how?" She looked wary about the idea.

"I mean, I have a ton of stuff to sort out back home, including but not limited to dealing with insurance for the car and also having enough internet to get started on finding the right architect for the job," I said.

I could have sworn she looked disappointed for a fraction of a second. "Sure, of course."

Well, this would work out perfectly. I smiled to myself, climbing into Flossie's truck.

"Okay, I know right now it's a little rough, but I want you to picture the rest of this sanded down and stained to a light oak color," I said, standing over the headboard. The bed was taken apart and was in a current state of half-goopy pink paint, half-unfinished wood. It was a stunning four poster with good bones and a lot to offer. We were standing in Flossie's converted second garage, surrounded by half-finished metalwork projects.

"What's wrong with my bed now?" Remi asked, her brow furrowed.

What I wanted to say: It's hideous. It's a log cabin, gigantic, ugly bed.

What I said: "*Nothing*, of course. This one would just suit your style so much better."

She shrugged. "And what style is that?"

I grabbed my phone to show her the mood board I had started to create for her bedroom. It was all light grays with accents of navy blue and dusty orange and spring green. It was fresh and modern, vibrant yet relaxing. I showed her a picture of how I envisioned the bed — a showcase piece, four tall but minimal posts at each corner.

She shrugged. "I mean, I like that a lot, but I don't see how this baby pink princess canopy bed is…" She pointed to the picture on my phone. "That."

"Do you trust me?" I asked, really laying the puppy dog eyes on thick. If it worked for Stormy, it could work for me.

Remi blinked. "I do, but—"

Flossie leaned against the wall, sighing. "It really is a monstrosity, isn't it?"

I turned, glaring at her. "Whose side are you on?"

"You know, beds with posters on the edge are really good for tying people up." She said it casually, as though she was pointing out a fact about trees or commenting on the weather.

I stared at her with wide eyes.

"If you're into that kind of thing," Flossie added, casually walking out of the workroom.

FLOSSIE DROVE up the road back to the house — it was slightly less treacherous without the downpour, but the horribly steep cliff to one side still did a number on my nerves.

"Why don't you guys believe in guardrails?" I muttered.

"You think guardrails are gonna keep a truck like Big Bertha from falling off the side?" Flossie leaned forward to pat the dash.

Remi was staring out the window. She'd been quiet since mentioning that she could take me back to Denver. Maybe she was dreading seeing her mother?

Of course I was slightly upset to leave Remi, but life couldn't go on being a fun unplugged vacation forever. I had work to do. And for this project, it would be a *lot* of work.

A truck slowed down going in the opposite direction and Flossie stopped beside it, rolling down her window.

The man in the other truck rolled down his window, giving us a friendly wave. "Hi Flossie." He peered curiously past her into the cab where Remi and I sat beside Flossie on the bench seat.

"Hi Jerry," Flossie said, tipping her imaginary hat.

Seeing a new neighbor, I had an idea. "Ask him if he knows anyone who might be missing Stormy," I whispered to her.

"Quick question, do you know anyone who has lost a dog in the last few days? A little brown beauty. Some kind of pit bull, I'd guess," Flossie said, leaning her elbow on the window frame.

The man thought for a minute. "You know, something is ringing a bell but I'm just not sure."

"Okay, well, if you hear anything, send them up to this tech kid's ranch. Peak 8, I think it's called?"

The man snorted. "Original."

Remi turned slowly, blinking. "Thanks," she said with a polite smile. "Named it myself."

Wow, Remi was hysterically powerless against the teasing of her neighbors, and I was unashamedly here for it.

"I'll check in with Justin and Monica and see if they can spread the word." Jerry said, nodding. He patted the outside of his truck. I fully expected him to say giddy up as he did it. "Well, have a nice day now."

Flossie saluted and drove forward.

"You're going to give away my dog?" Remi said, staring down at me.

"She's not yours. She's got to belong to someone." I rolled my eyes, but I was secretly a little touched at how quickly Remi had fallen in love with Stormy.

We drove over the planks in the road patching the part of the bridge that had fallen away. It wasn't the most stable situation, but we made it across and up the driveway.

"Thank you for the wonderful breakfast company," I

said to Flossie, giving her a hug as I scooted out of the truck.

"Anytime, dearie," she said, smiling. She turned to Remi, using two fingers to point to her own eyes, then towards Remi in an I'm-watching-you move.

Remi rolled her eyes and we walked inside.

We both agreed that we had a bit of work to catch up on and went our separate ways. Remi disappeared to an area of the house I suspected had a home office of some sort, and I wandered through the rooms taking pictures and jotting down ideas, then began to draft up a request for proposals from local architects. Stormy followed me from room to room.

I put on a record as I worked, surprised that Remi had Carole King's Tapestry, but grateful, nonetheless. I stared down at the record cabinet, a small, boring, boxy, vaguely midcentury thing. I started picturing the jars of paint sitting in my bag. It was a small piece in fine condition already, but with a little paint, it had a lot of potential.

I pulled the record player off the top, but kept Carole jamming, as I dragged the cabinet out to the back porch to get started.

Remi liked minimal and boring… what if I painted just the top two-thirds of the piece white? It'd retain some of the wooden charm and make an impact, but it'd look fresh, it'd pop against the Gray Wisp/Bunny Gray/Gray whatever walls we were planning on, and it'd keep me busy as I began to realize my time was limited.

Not limited, just… different. It was a little surprising how quickly I'd grown used to being here. The thought of leaving in the morning, even if I was going to return soon, made me feel unsettled.

I found some painters tape in the garage and got to work.

It was around three in the afternoon that I heard someone knock on the front door.

Stormy barked, wagging her tail only when she saw me beside her.

Remi appeared from Who Knows Where and opened the door while I stood directly behind her.

"Remington?" The man asked.

Remi nodded, her expression hardened.

Stormy barked, the sound sharp and piercing, before weaseling her way through my legs. She stood in front of me, wagging her tail tentatively.

"Kiki," the man said, kneeling down on the patio to welcome Kiki — formerly Stormy — into his arms.

She leaned forward and licked his face, but didn't seem overly excited to see him.

"I can't thank you enough. I really thought I lost her," he said, awkwardly patting her gigantic round head.

Remi cleared her throat. "Of course. She must have gotten out in the storm, so we were just doing what was right and keeping her safe until we could find you."

The man introduced himself as Nick, pointing to where he lived up the road. Apparently Justin had told Fred who told Heinrich who passed the message onto him.

Remi gave him her number, telling him that if he ever needed a dog sitter or anything, he could call.

As she shut the door, I could see that she was on the verge of tears.

"Kiki? She's not a Kiki," she whispered, her voice cracking.

Sympathy and adoration took over my body, and I wrapped my arms around her. I'd been wary of her since last night's fight, afraid she'd need more space. We both needed time to work out the next step. But seeing her start to cry, I held her, letting her rest her face in the crook of my shoulder.

"It's okay, she's with her family again. We should be happy," I said, even as a tear or two rolled down my own cheek.

She nodded, still sobbing.

"Maybe you should adopt a dog," I offered.

"No, Stormy was perfect," she whined.

Ah, so it was like that. I caressed her hair. "You need to relax. Do you want me to run a big bath in your terribly gaudy tub upstairs?"

She sniffled, nodding.

I paused to check the paint on the cabinet, then we walked upstairs and into the master bedroom. I just knew that four-poster bed would be gorgeous in here. I still had plenty of time to convince her, though. We'd be working on this project for a very long time to come, I was sure. It wasn't a small makeover.

I leaned over the tub, turning on the hot water. "Got any bath bombs?"

She shook her head.

"That's okay. Candles?"

She shook her head again, sniffling and mumbling about being bad at relaxing. Well, that much was clear already.

"Uh, alright," I said. "It'll be relaxing enough in this tub big enough for five grown adults to stretch out comfortably."

She laughed, sniffling again.

I tested the water temperature and stood, drying my hand on a towel. "Well, I'll leave you to it," I said.

She reached out and grabbed my wrist. "Wait," she said, looking up at me.

I paused, glancing from our hands to her.

"Care to join me?"

I smirked. Nice try.

"Please. Stay with me."

And I saw her as a scared, lonely, wounded person. Only this time, I wanted to be the salve that healed those wounds.

I nodded, and she stood, slipping her shirt over her head. I took my own shirt off, way less gracefully than she had, getting my head stuck in the neck, then my elbow in the arm. She lifted it the rest of the way for me.

We undressed in front of each other, and even though I'd seen her naked so many times before, and even recently in even more compromising positions, it felt strangely intimate, baring ourselves in front of the other.

I redid my ponytail to position it into a bun higher on top of my head, then climbed into the water. Remi followed and we perched on opposite ends, facing each other.

Once the tub was done filling, Remi reached over to shut off the water.

All was still and quiet.

"So," I started, unsure of what to say, but sure that the silence felt far too intense for my taste.

"Tell me something I don't know," she said, watching me curiously, those giant blue eyes reflecting the water back to me.

I paused, considering. "About?"

"You." She was so sure and confident in the response, I was almost taken aback.

"Oh, uh," I started. "I really like mustard on french fries."

She blinked, continuing her invasive stare. "I mean, tell me something about you I don't know. Tell me a secret you've never told anyone else."

"That's a little presumptuous," I said.

She moved, shifting her body over mine, her hands on the edge of the tub on either side of my head. "I think we're past the point of presumptions, Jude."

Why did my body come alive with the nearness of her? Every nerve ending in my entire being was tingling. I pressed my palms into my thighs to keep from reaching out to her.

"I think not graduating college was the best thing that ever happened to me," I said, speaking without thinking first.

She looked down at me. "Why?" She moved back, settling into the water, giving me space again.

"Because it forced me to figure out what I actually wanted to do with my life. I chose pre-med because it was a sure thing. A straight path forward. Med school, residency, doctor. But without it, I tried a whole bunch of different gigs. I was an event coordinator for one terrible summer. I worked in a bridal shop and cried every evening in the car on the way home for a year. And then I got really into refinishing furniture and interned with an interior designer whose style I admired, and the rest is... well, what led me here." I bit my lip, unsure how a woman with an MBA from MIT might take me being a struggling worker in a gig economy.

She raised her eyebrows. "You're the strongest woman I know. Your resiliency has always been incredible, but I'm really proud of you."

"Well, I couldn't have done any of it without the incredible ambition of a heartbroken woman who wanted to do anything to take her mind off of real life," I joked with a wink.

A pained expression crossed her face and she looked away.

"I'm sorry, that was... I meant that to be less dark than it came out."

She shrugged. "I deserve it."

I brushed a curl off of my forehead. "Tell me something I don't know."

"I'm thinking about leaving my father's company," she said quickly.

I nearly slipped under the surface of the water. "Whoa, that's kind of big."

She nodded. "I've been essentially running the airline on my own for years now. All those big plans he had for me were all so I would be the person in the office for him while he goes off and does god-knows-what. He wanted me to be his mini-me and I have been. Diligently taking on more and more of the responsibility, I'm gaining trust of the board, I've got concrete plans for expansion. And yet, I just want to destroy it. So, another place called, and... I don't know, I'm considering it."

"Why do you want to destroy your father's company?" I asked, curious. That seemed... bigger than she was letting on.

"Destroy is such a strong word. I just want to..." She paused, raking a wet hand through her hair, making it look wild. "Make him suffer for what he did. And originally I did want to just set fire to the whole thing, but now I think it will make him suffer more if I leave."

I tried to hide a surprised and alarmed expression.

"He took everything from us, Jude. Everything. He took *you* from me." Her brow pulled together and I thought she might start crying again. The last 24 hours could set a world record for the amount of times I'd ever seen Remington Van der Meer cry.

I nodded, trying to understand where she was coming

from. All that responsibility seemed so overwhelming. "Will leaving make you happy?"

She paused, looking contemplative. I could tell she was seriously warring with that thought.

"I'm not saying do it or don't do it," I hedged. "I just think it sounds like leaving might give you room to grow in a way that *you* want, not just what your parents want." I reached out, lacing my fingers in hers.

"I haven't let myself think that far." She reached for me, pulling me into her body, and all of my worries were suddenly far, far away.

I turned, sinking back into her strong body as her arms wrapped around me. She kissed the back of my neck, under my ear.

"It's just… Remember how happy we were?" She whispered.

I stilled. I'd spent so long suppressing those memories. It wasn't fair for her to stir them all up again without warning.

"What are you afraid of?" She asked.

My throat tightened with emotion. I rested my head back onto her hard chest. "All of it."

"All of what?"

I took a deep breath, steadying my nerves. It was easier to talk to her facing away, surrounded by the warmth of her. "What if you hurt me again? Or worse, what if we're happy, but we can never truly forgive each other for what happened ten years ago?"

"You're afraid to be happy?"

I chewed on my lower lip, trying to find the right word for it. "I'm afraid of the fragility of happiness."

"What do you mean?"

"On an average day, I'm pretty happy. I've created a

life for myself where I'm in control of how I feel for the most part." And I'd worked damn hard to get there.

"And you're afraid I'd mess that up?"

"You've already messed that up *so* much," I said with a laugh.

Her arms tightened around me and she pressed her cheek into my hair as I slid my hands up and down her legs — her naked body was a very good distraction. It was comforting to revel in the simple feeling of her body again.

"I mean, you're stubborn and alarmingly goal-oriented," I said, closing my eyes.

"And you're chaotic with a lot of sass," she said.

I grinned. She wasn't wrong.

She pressed kisses into my cheek and jawline.

"What if it doesn't work out between us?" I asked, opening my eyes again as I tilted my head to look up at her.

She took a deep breath, sighing. "But what if it *does*?"

My heart clenched at the innocent wonder of her eyes as she said it, and I knew in that moment, more than ever, more than back in our young and wild and impulsive days, that my heart would always belong to Remi. That wasn't in question.

A heart was such a fragile thing to begin with. Mine had broken into so many jagged pieces ten years ago. It didn't matter if she tried to be gentle — there was weakness in the seams. It was held together by nothing more than cheap glue and perseverance and never pausing to look over my shoulder. What if that meant I was unable to love her with the careless, complete abandon and trust she deserved?

CHAPTER TWELVE

OF ONE THING I WAS CERTAIN: I WAS GOING TO MAKE JULIA
trust in me again, and I didn't care how long that took.
Hours — preferable, but unlikely — days, weeks,
months... I'd spend the rest of my life assuring her, if she
needed me to.

But for now, I was content just being near her, simply
holding her in the bathtub. Running my hands over her
soft skin, the flare of her hips, the roundness of her thighs.
She was perfection, and I was happy just to spend the still,
quiet afternoon together.

It'd been a real rollercoaster of a day — hell, few days,
really. Julia had arrived on my doorstep and flipped my
entire world upside down.

I was fine before. I didn't need anyone. I didn't want
anyone.

And now? How was I going to let her leave tomorrow?

As if reading my mind, she took a deep breath. "How
long is your mom going to be here?"

We were lying naked in a warm, gigantic bathtub, and

she wanted to talk about my mother? I sighed, pulling my wandering hands away from her breasts in order to answer her properly.

"I'm not sure. She never stays for more than a few days. I think she must be bored," I said, shrugging.

Julia nodded. "That will be nice, though. Having her here."

Being around my mother was a mixed bag. I loved her, I trusted her, and yet, in person she always stressed me out. She was a very particular woman and did not appreciate changes to her routine — a truly hysterical hill to die on when visiting another person's home.

"Where did you live before?" She asked, her voice quieter.

"Chicago," I answered.

"Did you like it?"

"Not really," I answered truthfully. "It's a good base for the airline, but it's just so... packed." It was concrete and high-rises, though still undeniably better than New York or LA.

She nodded against my chest. "Ah, I bet you loved that." Was she grinning? I tried to study the look on her face.

"Sure did not," I said with a chuckle. "Why did you stay in Colorado after your parents left?"

"I'd never know which way was west if I left." She held up her hands. "I'm getting all pruny. Want to hop on out of here?"

"Only if we don't have to put on clothes." A pretty solid compromise, in my opinion.

She rolled her eyes. "You are shameless." She moved to climb out of the bathtub.

I grinned. "Fair, but I think you like it a little bit."

She reached for a towel, drying off her body as I watched.

"You gonna marinate for a bit longer?" She asked.

I shook my head, climbing out after her, a little hurt by the fact that she turned away as I did so until I noticed her watching me in the mirror. I winked at her reflection.

She laughed, throwing me a towel. "It shocks me how much you haven't changed. They let you run a company? You're sure about that?"

I grinned, my cheeks hurting from how much I was smiling around her lately. "Isn't it alarming? I still question it myself most days." I wrapped the towel around my waist.

"Why do you wear your towel like that?" She eyed my bare chest, her eyes slowly lowering to my hips again.

"It's too hot if I wrap it around my chest," I explained. "And it's not like I really have much to cover up here." My barely A-cup breasts were doing fine out on their own.

"It's just distracting." Her mouth quirked up at the edge in a smirk.

"Oh, is it?" I asked, stepping towards her.

She nodded. "I want to be polite and not stare at your chest, and yet, here we are." She made a show of looking down, then up again.

"You can do more than just stare, you know," I said, daring another step closer.

"Oh, is that so?" She whispered.

I reached and pulled the towel from around her, and before she could protest, I kissed her, pushing her backwards into the counter. Her kiss was soft and tentative — we'd been operating off of lust for the past three days, but now? Something new was lingering between us.

I reached to hook her leg around my hip, and as soon

as she followed suit with the other, I lifted her, carrying her out of the bathroom and to the bed.

I put a knee on the mattress, laying her gently back as I climbed on top of her. "Do you think we'll ever get tired of this?" I mumbled in between kisses.

She smiled against my mouth. "You've always been insatiable."

"Oh, you're pinning this all on me?" I teased.

"I'm completely innocent." She laughed, and I wanted to bottle the sound to have later — pure joy with a touch of mischief and teasing.

I reached between her legs, feeling just how wet she was. "Oh, yeah, I see this is very one-sided," I said, circling her clit once before raising my hand again.

She looked at my fingers with an intrigued expression, then looked back to my face. While holding her intense eye contact, I slipped my finger inside of my mouth, the sweet taste of her making me moan slightly.

Her lips parted in surprise, then her expression turned hungry. She fisted a hand in my hair, pulling me down to kiss her. Her tongue swept over mine, and I knew she could taste herself there. The thought made me moan again.

Something shifted in the air around us. Something that hadn't been there in the kitchen or the back patio. It was in the slowness in our movements, the gentleness of our touch, the way her eyes stared into mine — not with determination, but with vulnerability.

We laid in bed for hours, returning to something so familiar yet entirely ineffable.

JULIA HAD STILL BEEN DOZING in my bed when I got up, my

stomach rumbling. It was already 8pm by the time I
wandered back downstairs.

I fixed dinner, the orzo pesto I'd found in the cabinet
before. I had put on music, slow and calming. I was setting
the table and lighting candles when she walked down the
stairs wearing nothing but one of my oversized sweat-
shirts. Her ginger curls looked wild, and I thought about
forgetting dinner altogether.

"Ooh, food?" She asked, looking from me to the
candles.

I cleared my throat. "Julia Evans, will you do me the
honor of staying in for dinner with me?" I desperately
wanted to wine and dine her, to make her see that we
could be good together again.

She smiled. "Sounds lovely." She fussed with her hair
for a moment before I reached for her.

"You look incredible. Did it take you long to get ready?"
I asked, pulling her in to wrap my arms around her.

She genuinely laughed at that, and I cherished each
wrinkle that appeared at the corners of her eyes. I kissed
the tip of her nose, then her forehead.

I popped open a bottle of Perrier I'd had stashed in the
cupboard and poured it into two wine glasses.

"You are ridiculous, but I don't hate it," she said,
taking the wine glass and settling into a chair.

We talked over dinner and it felt so natural. Nothing
with Julia felt forced, but it all felt different than it had. So
much of her was familiar, but so much was new. I was
excited to learn everything about her, all over again.

After dinner was over, we sat on the patio, cuddled
into a lounge chair together.

The night air was crisp, and I tucked the edge of the
blanket further around Julia's shoulder.

She let out a sigh and I brushed a curl away from her face. "What's on your mind?"

"I don't know if I can continue the project if we're... I don't know how to phrase it. Doing this. If we plan to do this. I don't want to presume, I just..." She made a point to look anywhere but at me.

"Slow down," I said calmly. I shifted so that my body was angled towards hers. "Now, let's take that one bit at a time."

"What is this?" She asked, chewing on her lip. She was looking down.

I reached to lift her chin with my fingers, forcing her to look at me. "You know what it is."

Her brow furrowed. "Do I?"

"This is what we were always meant to have." I was so sure. I wanted to shake her by the shoulders to force her out of that overcomplicated mind and thought process of hers.

"But what is it exactly?" She asked again.

"What do you want it to be?" I leaned forward, touching my nose to hers. I couldn't resist the closeness of her now. We had so much lost time to make up for.

"Are we dating? Am I your girlfriend?"

I tried to suppress a laugh. "Why does any of that matter?" We had so much more than a label could define.

Her nose wrinkled in the most adorable display of indignation I'd ever seen. "It matters to me. Yesterday we could barely stand each other, and now?"

"Everything changed for me last night. Did nothing change for you this morning?"

"Of course it changed, but we're different people than we were ten years ago."

I nodded. She was right up to a point. "I think we're

the same people at our cores, though. I still feel like you know me better than anyone," I said.

"Only because you don't let anyone in." Her eyes were wide with question.

I took her hand and kissed her palm. "I let you in."

She softened at that. "I just don't want to jump straight to marriage or something."

I did laugh at that, finally. I frowned in amusement. "Who said anything about marriage?"

"So, we'll never get married?"

Good god, the emotional whiplash of this woman. I needed a massage. I pressed into the tension knots of my shoulders.

"Baby, let's take this one step at a time. I want to be with you. Let's start there. Do you want to be with me?"

"In what way?"

Wow, she really was serious about how badly she needed a label. I took a deep breath, considering my options. "I don't want to be with anyone else, and I don't want you to be with anyone else. If you'd like to call me your girlfriend, I'd be okay with that. If you'd rather call me your partner, or your person, or your main squeeze, or your side chick, I don't care."

"Side chick does have a nice ring to it," she said with a small smirk. She leaned forward, kissing the tip of my nose. "I think I can live with that for now."

I grinned and pressed a firm kiss to her lips. "Okay, that settles that part. It's you and me against the world, Evans."

"About that," she began, her voice wary again.

I tilted my head, looking down to her face. Dread pooled in my stomach.

"I meant it about the project. I don't want this thing just because I'm your person. I want this project because

I'm the best choice. And even then, is it really appropriate for you to be overpaying me for it?" She sighed. She'd clearly worried about this quite a bit.

Well, that was adorable.

"First, I liked your vision. I trust whatever you have in store. I'm game, because you know me, and I think you know what I'll like." I tried to catch her eyes to make her realize I was being sincere. "Baby pink princess beds aside."

"That bed will be fantastic, I promise."

"I can afford a new bed if that's what you're worried about."

"That's not exactly a sustainable solution, Rem. Besides, it's more fun to repurpose and reuse what's already out in the world."

I hugged her tighter. "I trust you and your vision." Was it possible to love her any more? Whoa, that was a big word. I meant adore. Definitely just adore.

"I don't typically sleep with my clients, though. Don't you think there's kind of a line we're crossing here?" Her forehead wrinkled in concern.

"*Typically*? You've slept with your clients before?"

She widened her eyes innocently. "None of your business."

I gasped in faux-surprise, reaching to tickle her waist.

She giggled — *giggled!* — and struggled against my attack, gasping for breath. "Stop it," she commanded, which made me tickle her more.

I only let up when the whining began.

"Let's find a compromise." She took a deep breath, completely back to business as normal.

"Oh? And that would be?" I reached to cup her face in my hand, brushing my thumb against the soft skin of her cheek.

"Either you consider other designers and choose which presentation you like best, or we don't tell anyone we're dating during the project. I want to be taken seriously." She had a determined look on her face.

"Judith," I began.

"Don't you dare," she whispered, glaring at me.

"Judy." I tried to stop grinning.

Her eyes narrowed into menacing slits. "I will call the chipmunks with switchblades out here to end you right now."

What the hell was she talking about? Anyway, I wasn't done. "Hey, Jude," I sang.

She rolled her eyes.

"I just want you to realize that I'm done considering anything but you. So, if you want to keep it secret during the design and construction, your wish is my command." Even though I didn't like the idea, it seemed to settle her nerves in the moment.

She sighed, considering it. "Okay. But, one other thing."

Anything. I looked at her, letting her know she had my attention and waited for her to continue.

"Donate that $100k to the local nonprofit Flossie mentioned earlier. The one cleaning up the town." She smiled up at me.

I blinked, too surprised to say anything. "You don't want me to pay you? At all?"

"No, it doesn't feel right, Rem," she said. "That money is needed elsewhere."

The damage to Breckenridge had haunted me since I had really taken it in that morning. Downed trees, downed power lines, flooded roads, damaged historical buildings. It was awful.

"Plus, decorating this house will be a personal project,

too, won't it? I'll still use it in my portfolio, which is what I wanted in the first place."

"How about this? We call the money I was going to give you a donation from you, and then I match it with my own donation?" I said. That way, we'd get to double our impact, and Julia could feel proud of it, too. I'd find another way to pay her for her time. Maybe a less obvious one.

Now it was her turn to be surprised. She stared up at me with wide eyes. "Really? You'd do that?"

I nodded.

"You always have a sneaky way of supporting people without them realizing, don't you?" She asked, smiling slyly.

I raised a brow. "What do you mean?"

"Well, your friend's surgery fund, and now this?"

I rolled my eyes.

"I knew it," she said, grinning like she had found out my deepest secret. "You're *good*. You act all tough and begrudging, but you're good."

I faked a grimace, my cheeks flushing with very real embarrassment. "Don't slander me."

She laughed. "Sure, baby, you can keep on acting all tough."

We stayed still on the lounge chair for a long while, listening to the crickets, the cicadas, the night breeze through the valley below. The citronella torches kept the patio aglow in comforting light.

A strange noise caught my attention, and I realized it was quiet footsteps on the patio stairs. My adrenaline kicked up almost immediately as I stilled, listening. Not wanting to alarm Julia, I tried to lift my head to see what was coming for us.

"What is it?" She asked, her head still on my chest.

The footsteps were growing closer, and I could definitely make out that they weren't a human. What the hell animal would climb the stairs so quietly?

I sat up fully, ready to grab whatever I could use as a weapon or large object to scare away an animal, completely prepared for the aforementioned switchblade-wielding chipmunks, when Stormy's head popped over the last stair. She wagged her tail and her face split into a large smile, her tongue lolling out.

"Oh my god," Julia said, holding a hand to her chest. She called Stormy to her.

Stormy wiggled across the patio, jumping up onto the lounger with us, which only managed to tip us backwards. We fell into a heap of limbs, laughing as we cried out in surprise.

I wrapped my arms around Stormy. "You shouldn't be here," I told her, hugging her close. "But I'm glad you are."

"It's pretty late," Julia said, taking a deep breath. "She should probably just stay the night until we can take her back to Nick's tomorrow morning."

"Yeah, that's clearly the only thing to do," I said with a knowing smile.

We made our way up to bed, and I gripped Julia's hand to lead the way to my own bedroom. We brushed our teeth, changed into pajamas, and snuggled under the covers. Stormy sprawled out at our feet. It was a simple scene, but to me, it was everything.

CHAPTER THIRTEEN

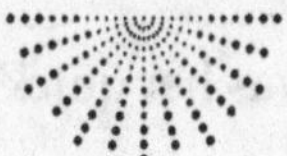

JULIA

"AND YOU'RE *SURE* WE WON'T DIE?" I ASKED, STARING AT THE small plane in the hangar. It was tiny — Remi had explained what it was but all I heard was "Cessna" and "fast."

"I promise you won't die," Remi said, shaking her head.

We'd checked in at a front desk and received a copy of our filed flight plans that Remi's assistant had logged the day before.

The plane itself was kind of an adorable shape — it definitely had a nose and therefore a personality. It was sleeker than I imagined a Cessna being, and it was painted with yellow and gray stripes. Remi lifted the door for me, tossed my bags inside and then pointed to the step in front of the wing, boosting me up.

I climbed in, taking in the interior. The seats were a stylish beige leather, buttery under my hand. In front of me was an entire dash panel of screens and colored buttons. I leaned my elbow on the center console and a loud beep sounded. I jerked my arm away to find that there was a screen beside me, too.

100% Death Trap.

Remi walked around the plane with a checklist in her hand, inspecting things and looking generally important.

I sent a text to Cameron. "About to be in a small plane. Pray for me."

"What the what?" was her quick reply, which seemed about right.

It was less than an hour's flight, but we'd gotten up at the crack of dawn for it regardless. Apparently Remi was meeting her mother around 8 at a small airport west of Denver. She seemed more nervous than usual that morning as we climbed out of bed — she wouldn't even let me distract her for a quickie to remember me by.

We'd dropped off Stormy at Nick's house, who seemed equally confused and upset to see that Stormy — "Kiki" as he so incorrectly called her — had disappeared again. Hadn't he noticed?

We'd driven to the airport in silence, my stomach a ball of nerves both from the having to leave Rem and the flying.

She assured me that I'd love it, but clearly she didn't know me at all.

I kept my arms close to my body as I looked around. Damn, there was a pretty roomy backseat in this thing. If we weren't on such a tight timeline... I was just about to reach out and touch a button when Remi scolded me from the open door of the other side.

"Don't touch anything," she said, looking more amused than upset.

I jumped, tucking my hands between my thighs for safekeeping.

The sun had lightened the sky, but hadn't yet crested the mountains to the east of Breck.

Remi climbed in beside me and handed me a pair of sunglasses from a compartment near her left knee. "You're gonna want these."

"So, I'm going to be steering and you're going to be navigating, do I have that right?" I joked, reaching for another lever.

She smacked my wrist playfully. "No, you're going to be watching in awe and amazement from that seat, not touching anything unless I tell you to." She smirked.

"I think you're undervaluing my skills."

"I'm sure I am," she said, glancing behind us, then staring up at the levers and buttons on the ceiling. She handed me a pair of headphones, then put her own on.

Remi mumbled a bunch of words into the radio, all of which I recognized individually but couldn't make sense of together. Her voice was hysterically Pilot-esque over the radio, even slightly fuzzy in a familiar way. I fully expected her to say the words "Niner niner." She pressed a few more buttons, and the plane tipped forward. The propeller started to move on the nose, and we began moving.

I gripped my thighs, the only place I felt safe putting my hands.

Remi continued to talk into the radio, but I was staring out the window, trying to will my heart to slow down before it beat out of my chest.

"I will never let anything happen to you, Jude," Remi said through the headset and I looked sideways at her. She winked, pressing more buttons as we crept out of the hangar area and onto a series of small runways.

"Okay, you ready?" She asked as we paused. The plane

was humming beneath me, way louder than I would have suspected.

I nodded, swallowing.

"If you're nervous, watch the screens. They won't lie to you," she said.

The screens in front of me had two views — one was an overhead map of the airport and projected flight path. The other was a simulated version of the runway ahead of us.

She grinned, and then we were off, speeding down the runway. My stomach lodged itself somewhere between my lungs and throat, and I tried to resist closing my eyes.

At 120 miles per hour, the front wheel lifted from the ground, then the back, and we began to ascend. I wanted to focus on the screens, but I was surprisingly transfixed by the view out the window.

The ground seemed to move away so quickly. According to the screens, we were taking off at nearly 1000 ft per minute. I popped my ears, watching the town turn into a tiny diorama village.

"The house is right over there," Remi pointed to the right, and I nearly pressed my face against the window, trying to make it out.

"I think I see Flossie's, but not yours," I said, squinting.

"Good." She laughed. "That means no pilots can creep on what you do to me on that back porch."

I laughed. "You did not just say that."

I watched her hold the controls steady, pressing buttons when they were needed. She pressed a few buttons between us, explaining that she was changing the frequency. Her total competency and ability to do complex things was a strange thing to find attractive, but here I was, nearly drooling over her. I tore my eyes away, watching the scenery below.

I wasn't a good flyer, but that didn't mean I didn't

enjoy looking at the world from above. Everything looked so carefully constructed, each mountain peak carved from clay.

"Watch your eyes, babe," she warned, and suddenly the sun was almost directly in my eyes.

She explained that she was switching it over the autopilot, and then leaned back in her seat, watching the screens with intensity.

The flight passed with relative ease. No major bumps made me want to lose my breakfast of an oat bar and dried mango slices I'd found in the Jeep's glove compartment.

"So, you still think this is so bad?" She asked, turning to me after about a half hour.

I shook my head. "No, I think it's actually easier than flying in a normal airplane, because you can explain to me what's going on. Plus, watching you be a pilot is unbelievably sexy."

She laughed. "Oh yeah?" She waggled her eyebrows in a silly gesture.

"So how 'autopilot' is the autopilot?" I asked, gesturing to the backseat. "You want to christen this thing?" I winked.

She laughed again, shaking her head. "You're shameless, but I did promise not to kill you, so I'm going to have to pass on that for now."

"Zero fun," I said, crossing my arms over my chest in a faux-pout.

With each mile we passed, the realization that I'd be leaving her began to sink in. All I had wanted was to return to Denver, get home, get my life back in order, but now that it was happening, it felt a bit bittersweet.

"I'm going to miss you," I said.

She reached over and squeezed my knee. "I'm going to miss you. Get the car thing figured out and then come back to me, deal?" She had a peculiar look on her face that I couldn't quite place.

"Get your internet back before making any real demands." I rolled my eyes.

"Touché. How about we work on both of these ventures simultaneously?"

"I think I can live with that." I nodded, watching out the window. I was afraid that if I looked at her for too long, I'd start tearing up, knowing that our little bubble was bursting.

What a wild ride the past few days had been. My entire life had been upended by one phone call from Remi's assistant. She really deserved a raise, in my opinion.

Remi spoke over the radio again, confirming her plans for landing, and then lined herself up with the runway. We hit a burst of turbulence and my stomach flipped up again.

The plane leveled out and tiny blades flipped out of the wing — she explained they were speed brakes, but I was convinced they looked more like throwing stars than anything that deserved to be on a plane. We descended quickly, and I popped my ears about four thousand more times.

Then, in one smooth swoop, we were on the runway. The force pushed me back into my seat as we slowed.

"Look at how alive we are," Remi said, turning to me.

I laughed. "Fine, fine, you win this round, Van der Meer, but don't think this is the end of it. I'll be back and you'll be sorry."

I watched a grin spread on her face as she navigated the plane to its designated spot on the tarmac, out of the way.

As the plane stopped, Remi hopped out and walked around the front, coming to my side to help me down.

My foot slipped on the step and I flopped into her arms in a sheer mastery of elegance.

"She's beauty and she's grace," Remi teased, setting me on the ground. She held me, pressing light kisses to my lips.

"Remington?" A woman's voice sounded behind us. Her thick Southern accent, flawless hair, and expensive looking shoes left no guess about who she was — Remi's mother.

Remi turned, keeping her arm around my waist until her mother stepped up with her arms outstretched for a hug. "You're early," Remi said, but she was smiling.

I awkwardly watched Remi hug her mother, not knowing if I should introduce myself or stay out of the way. I settled for staying out of the way until her mother's eyes landed on me, looking me up and down with curiosity.

Remi glanced between us.

"Mom, this is Julia, a friend of mine. Julia, this is my mother, Emily," Remi said quickly, gesturing between us.

"Emily, so nice to meet you," I said, reaching out to shake her hand.

She gave me a limp wrist, letting me clutch her fingers in the world's most awkward handshake. "Lovely to meet you," she said warmly.

Maybe I had just misinterpreted the weird vibe. She seemed nice enough, save for her lack of handshake skill.

"Okay, well, I'll be in touch," I said awkwardly to Remi. Did I hug her? Did I kiss her? I settled for a high-five, really leaning into being terribly uncomfortable.

She laughed, catching my hand. She leaned down and kissed me. "I'll text you when we land back home," Remi said, giving me a small salute and wink. "I already arranged for a car for you. It should be at the terminal."

She reached back into the plane and pulled out my bags, handing them to me. She looked from her mother to me as if to apologize for not being able to walk me to the car.

"Okay," I said, waving. Remi pointed me towards the small terminal.

Emotion made my throat feel thick and tight as I tried to swallow the rising sadness. I knew it would only be a week or so until I saw her again, but I'd thought that the last time I left her.

I turned over my shoulder and watched Remi help her mother into the seat I had just been in.

Disappointment and anxiety waged war inside of my chest as I walked through the terminal, grateful for the oversized sunglasses Remi had given me in the plane that I had absolutely stolen without a second thought.

Parked in front of the terminal was an SUV, but it was empty. I looked around. Maybe the car was late. I leaned against a railing, waiting.

After ten minutes, I was starting to grow frustrated. I just wanted to go home and cry into my own pillow, wallowing in self-pity and listening to Taylor Swift's newest breakup album in the dark until Remi confirmed that she was, indeed, still talking to me.

I walked back inside the terminal and headed for the desk.

"Hi, this is going to sound weird, but there's supposed to be a car for me. Julia Evans? Or if you have no idea what I'm talking about, I can just call an Uber," I said, uncomfortably rambling.

The receptionist smiled at me, then her eyes widened as I said my name. "Oh, I'm so sorry Miss Evans. I was meant to stop you as you walked through the first time, but I must have just missed you," she said, though I was a little distracted by her absolutely flawless lipstick, which seemed unfair at 7:30am. She handed me a set of keys. "Here you go."

I stared down at the keys in my palm. "I think there's been a mistake?" I tried to hand them back.

"Yours is the only one parked right in front," she pointed with a smile.

Was it a rental? I thanked her politely even though I knew she was completely incorrect and walked outside, eyeing the car suspiciously as though it might be a prank of some sort.

I hit the unlock button on the key fob and heard the door locks click. I opened the front door slowly, feeling wary of what I might find inside.

Did it seem slightly ridiculous that I was expecting the worst out of a random car? Sure. Was I going to act any braver in this moment? Nope.

I climbed into the car and looked around. There was a note on the passenger seat. I knew I was right to be wary — something really weird was going on here.

I picked up the note, flipping it over in my hand. It was unfamiliar handwriting, but who else would have left a Neruda poem for me?

"I who lived in a harbor from which I loved you.
The solitude crossed with dream and with silence.
Penned up between the sea and sadness.
Soundless, delirious, between two motionless gondoliers.
Jude, let's just enjoy the ride. Love, Remi."

I gasped, throwing the note as though it had just bitten me. "Oh my god," I said aloud, looking around the car a little more carefully. It was a brand new luxury SUV and it must have been the nicest package — the most *expensive* package by a mile.

A tiny angel version of myself appeared on my left shoulder. "There's no way you can keep this car, Julia."

A tiny devil appeared on my right shoulder. "You're *so* keeping this car. *And* she said *love*."

"She did say love," the angel agreed. "But this is an expensive gift, and you're above accepting this. You want her for more than her money."

"Ah, but the money is a perk," the devil agreed. "It's a gift. It'd be rude not to accept it. Plus, check out that poem. Just like old times."

"No way. You have to give it back." The angel threw up her arms, exasperated. "This is *not* just like old times."

I shook my head, clearing the tiny angel and devil from my mind. Wow, the lack of oxygen from the plane ride must have gotten to me.

I stared at the dashboard of the car. I'd just use it until I could get mine repaired. I wasn't going to keep it forever, but it was a kind favor, and who was I to look a gift girlfriend in the mouth?

I turned the engine and the car purred to life. Oh no. Somewhere in my imagination, tiny devil Julia was fist pumping the air, and tiny angel Julia was shaking her head in disbelief.

I drove home, excited to feel completely in control for the first time since driving up the road to Remi's house.

As I walked in the front door of my house, exhaustion took over my body. I hadn't realized how drained I was. I made it to the couch and had just enough time to text Remi, "You think you're slick with this whole car and love thing." before promptly falling asleep.

I awoke several hours later to seven missed calls from Cameron and a few texts from Remi telling me she'd made it to the airport, then back home. To my annoyance, she didn't say anything about the car *or* the love thing. Then another with photographic evidence that Stormy had reappeared on the porch, making herself very much at home in a sunny spot on the back deck.

I sent a heart eyes emoji to Remi before calling Cameron back.

"Did your house burn down?" I asked, confused. "What's with all the calls?"

"No, you said you'd let me know once you got back to Denver, and then I didn't hear from you, and then I thought your tiny plane crashed, and then I was looking up hospitals along the I-70 corridor to call to check on you." She sounded exasperated and tired.

"I'm sorry, my dude. You okay?" I asked.

She took a deep breath. "Yeah, I will be."

"You're never going to guess who that client was." I said, biting my lower lip. I stood, pacing around my small house, tidying up and watering plants as I spoke.

"Wait, do we know your client?"

"Yep," I said.

"How do we both know like any of the same people?" She began in skeptical disbelief.

"It's someone we know from a long time ago," I hinted.

"Someone we went to college with? Someone we like?"

"Ehhh, like is a loose term. Think of the person least likely to reappear in our lives."

She paused, considering. "It isn't."

"It most definitely is the worst case scenario."

"She-Who-Must-Not-Be-Named?"

I laughed. "The very one."

"Satan Incarnate."

I laughed harder.

"Why aren't you more upset right now?" She asked, sounding alarmed.

"Well, it gets... interesting."

I paced, explaining the entire trip from start to finish, though I left out a few key details involving countertops and patio lounge chairs. By the end of the story, Cameron was yelling in disbelief and shock.

"You know what? I'm coming over," she said.

I grinned. "Sure, I'll see you in however long it takes to fly from Minneapolis to Denver."

I heard clicking on a keyboard.

"Oh, you think I'm joking," she said, sounding slightly distracted.

"Wait—" I still had a ton of work to do. I still had to meet with the list of architects I'd narrowed down.

"Okay, my flight gets in at 6pm." She said in her signature just-fucking-try-to-argue-with-me tone.

I couldn't help but feel giddy with excitement. I hadn't seen Cameron in nearly six months, when I'd gone up to the Twin Cities to visit her the last time. "You're something else," I said.

"I hope you're ready to have a serious intervention. And maybe some Taco Bell." She took a deep breath and sighed.

CHAPTER FOURTEEN

REMINGTON

"It's so kind of you to call me," I said, raking a hand nervously through my hair.

"No problem, I'll make this quick. We'd love to have you come meet the board early next week, if you'd be okay with that," Steven said, and I nodded involuntarily. He was the Chair of the Board — the recruiter had put us in touch directly. The same recruiter that had only given me a ten minute heads up that the Chair of the Board of Guardian Airlines was going to be calling me.

"I can absolutely make that happen." That'd be perfect — it gave me an excuse to have my mother leave after only a few short days and then I'd be able to see Julia, too.

"Perfect. I'll arrange it with your assistant," Steven said.

I tried to lower the enthusiasm in my tone so as not to seem too desperate. I couldn't have them thinking it was a done deal or I'd never get anything I really wanted in the negotiations.

Mom smirked at me from across the living room. I'd

been caught off guard by Steven's call and hadn't been able to go somewhere more private.

I'd already walked her through the whole house, Stormy at our heels, as I tried to explain Julia's vision. I wished Julia was here to explain it herself — the words "minimal luxury" sounded so dumb coming from my mouth, but Julia knew exactly how to make it sound perfect. Mom didn't quite "get" it, but I was sure she'd get on board as soon as she saw it with her own eyes. And if she didn't, well, it wasn't her house anyway.

I grinned, looking down at my phone. I shot Julia a text saying I'd be in Denver Monday or Tuesday.

Julia: Cool, let me know what hotel you pick.

My brow furrowed in confusion. She wasn't just going to have me stay with her?

Julia: omg, I can see you scowling from here. Of course you can stay with me. Hope you like cozy!

I grinned again.

"Was it good news?" Mom asked.

"Hmm?"

"What are you smiling about now?" Her own smile was slightly tight.

"Guardian wants to meet with me early next week," I said. I was nervous just saying the words aloud. I blew out a puff of air, my hair flipping up in its wake.

"About the Osprey buyout?" She asked, her interest clearly piqued.

"Not exactly," I said. "Can I tell you something in confidence? As my mother? Not as a Board member?" God, the blurred lines of business and family were difficult to navigate sometimes.

I'd been relieved to see my mother again. I had been anxious for her trip, but from the moment she'd started copiloting the plane on the way home, I was grateful she was here. She'd been the one who taught me how to fly in the first place — most people assumed I'd gotten it from my father, but the man had never been a pilot. It had been my mom's infectious enthusiasm for flying that had led him to get involved in and eventually start his own airline at all.

I relayed the events of the past few days, how the recruiter had called me out of nowhere, how I was miserable thinking of working with my father, how I didn't think revenge was a good enough reason to push the company into a new territory.

"Do you think it's a bad move to leave EA? I know the company would be mine in fifteen years anyway, but I just don't think I can last that long with him." I said honestly, sitting down on a barstool.

Mom helped herself to my wine fridge, standing in silence as she scored the foil and rotated the screw in, then lifted the cork out. It opened with a satisfying pop sound. She held a glass up in question and I nodded.

"If there's anyone who can sympathize about not wanting to be around your father, it's me," Mom said with a grin, passing me a glass. That... was not the answer I expected.

I held my wine up in a cheers.

"But, I do just want to say that maybe the door is not closed to you still taking over EA someday. This experience at Guardian could very well be just the thing to convince future investors you're right for the job if the opportunity came along."

Something in her voice made me consider that perhaps this wasn't the first time she'd thought of this idea. Or maybe I was only inferring that because she was still a major investor in my father's airline after she'd inherited the 20% that her parents had purchased to help Dad even start the airline. Of course she'd have the company's interests at heart.

I held my tongue, taking a sip of the buttery Chardonnay.

"I am disappointed, of course," she said, still smiling. "But I only want what's best for you, darling. And then, when you're ready, you can come back to EA."

How about *never*?

Somehow I didn't think she'd enjoy that answer. The woman had stayed married to my dad for appearances only — she had ingrained such a sense of duty in me from the time I'd been a child that I'd never thought to question it. Hell, I still sometimes found myself not questioning it.

A knock at the door startled me. I crossed the foyer and looked out the side window. Flossie stood on the porch.

I sighed, not wanting to get caught up in any more neighborly drama.

"I can see you," Flossie said, catching my eye through the window.

I resisted the urge to smirk and say, "So?" Instead, I opened the door.

Flossie walked in immediately, her bedazzled cowboy boots clicking on the hardwood floor.

"Sure, come on in," I said, and stepped back.

"Did Kiki run back here?" Flossie asked, looking around the foyer.

Stormy walked casually into the room, eyeing up Flossie, looking extremely nonchalant about her presence in my house.

"Listen, this is getting out of hand," Flossie started. "I've convinced Nick that I could pick her up this time, but next time, he's just going to have to talk to you about it."

"Talk to me about what?" I asked, curious.

"I know you like her, but you can't just keep things

because you like them. Sometimes you have to make sure they are right for you. That you're right together." Flossie said, petting Stormy behind the ears.

She wasn't talking about Stormy, was she?

My mother appeared behind me.

Flossie looked surprised, looking between us. "Well, the apple doesn't fall far from the tree. Y'all could be sisters," Flossie said.

I looked back at my mother, who had dark hair and dark eyes. Sisters, sure.

Wait… was Flossie hitting on my mother?

I narrowed my eyes as my mother stepped in front of me, positively eating it up. She held out her hand. "I'm Remington's mother, Emily."

Flossie shook her hand. "Well," Flossie said, tipping the brim of her bowler hat towards my mother.

I held Stormy's leash in my hand, gripping the braided cord.

"There's a reason she keeps coming back. She likes it here, and I want her to be here. So, give me Nick's number," I said.

"You can't just have things because you want them." Flossie raised her eyebrows. "Have you stopped to consider if you're even right for her?"

Mom stood next to me, watching the exchange like a tennis match.

"When things are meant to be, it's only right to fight for them," I said.

Yep, we most certainly weren't talking about Stormy. I clenched the leash in my hand.

"I'm going to talk to Nick about this, like I should have done the first time she came back," I added, just to keep us on track.

Flossie winked at me, then took her phone out of her pocket, giving me Nick's number.

"Good luck, child," she said. Then, I watched in surprise as Flossie turned on her heel and sauntered out of the foyer.

"What on earth was that all about?" Mom asked, looking between me, Stormy, and the door.

"I have to make a call," I said, taking a deep breath.

I walked into the front sitting area, a room I never spent any time in, and dialed Nick's number. He picked up on the third ring.

"Hi Nick, it's Remington Van der—"

"Ah, hi Remington. Flossie called to say she was going to pick up Kiki, I think. Everything okay?" He sounded slightly wary.

"No, everything is not okay," I said firmly. "The dog keeps—"

"It's been stressing me out so much that she wants to be there with you. I know it's such a pain in the ass." He sighed loudly.

"No, that's just it. It's not a pain at all. She's *very* welcome here." I tried to make my point clear without making a demand.

Nick sighed again. He was deflating on the other end of the line. "She was my daughter's dog, and when Jessie went away to college, well Kiki has never quite taken a shine to me, no matter what I do. It's been four years now, and Jessie says she doesn't have room or time for a dog."

"Listen, why don't you just talk to your daughter and let me know if she'd be okay with me, uh," I paused, looking for the right word. "Adopting her dog?" I didn't want to just presume. "Please, pass along my number. She's welcome to call. And until you hear back, I can keep an eye on.... Kiki." Ugh, the name was so not Stormy. "You can call me anytime, day or night."

"I think I already know her answer will be yes, but I'll give her a call."

We hung up, and I stared down at my phone. My mom poked her head around the corner of the doorway. "Who was that?"

I looked down at Stormy who watched me with mild interest, but stayed beside me, wagging her tail. Excitement bubbled up inside of me. I knelt down, rubbing her ears.

"Well, I think I just got a dog," I said. First order of business: Dog food. And a bed. And a collar. And maybe a few more beds. Should I convert one of the bedrooms officially into Stormy's room? How would Julia decorate that?

Was I jumping in a little fast without having the official go-ahead? Probably. Was that going to stop me? Probably not.

"Want to run an errand with me?" I asked Mom.

She shook her head. "No, thank you. But I'll be fine here. I'm a bit tired from traveling earlier anyway. I think I'll go lie down while you're out."

I nodded. "Well, Stormy, want to come?" I asked excitedly. She stood, wiggling up at me. I couldn't wait to tell Julia the good news.

Stormy and I walked to the Jeep and I boosted her into the passenger seat.

"Pilot to copilot," I mimicked a radio in front of my mouth. She watched me curiously. "Are you ready for takeoff?" I idly wondered how she'd do in the plane as we wound our way down the mountain and into town.

I felt guilty for secretly enjoying the fact that I had a break from my mother for an hour or so. I enjoyed her company, but I felt like there was an underlying tension about the job change. She had a vested interest in me staying at Express, and I was old enough to realize that she wanted me there because that gave her more control, both over me and the company.

Simultaneously, didn't she want me to grow? She'd been the one who convinced my father all those years ago about my plan to go to McManus.

I had applied to the small liberal arts college behind their backs — I'd also applied to the schools they wanted me to due to family ties. Cornell, Michigan, even Princeton, though I knew I'd never fit in there. But I'd toured McManus on a whim when I was skiing in Vail, and I fell in love.

"Is this your dream?" Mom had asked, staring me down like some kind of FBI interrogator.

"It is. I want to fly under the radar. I want to be Remi, not just a Van der Meer. And I want space from Dad," I'd said, tying and untying my ponytail.

"You can never get away from the Van der Meer name, darling," she'd said. "And it is as much a gift as a burden. You'll see that someday."

I didn't understand her then, but I understood her perfectly now.

When we returned home, I found Mom sitting outside on the back deck, her back to me. I set Stormy's new haul down in the great room and opened the sliding glass door.

"She has returned," she said dramatically, smiling at me. She patted the lounge next to her.

"I was gone for an hour, I hardly think we can start calling me the prodigal daughter." I sat, taking the folded throw blanket, tossing it over my legs.

"So, tell me about the woman from the plane earlier," Mom smiled knowingly.

I blushed, feeling suddenly bashful about admitting it. Mom had seen me in college, how excited I was about Julia, how I never stopped talking to and about her. And she was the first person I showed the cheating pictures to. The first person to console me. To help me move on.

"You're never going to believe this, but it's my college girlfriend."

Stormy walked out onto the porch to join us and climbed into the lounge beside me, as if there was room.

"You had so many, dear. Which one?" Mom said, still smiling.

I rolled my eyes and laughed. "I did *not*. This was the only one that mattered. I know you know who I'm talking about."

Mom relaxed back in her chair, taking a sip of her sparkling water. "What did you say her name was?"

"Sure, play coy, Emily," I teased. "It's Julia."

"Julia," Mom said slowly, as if trying the word out for the first time.

"Anyway, such a weird coincidence, but she's my interior designer. Kelly hired her. Such a small world, right?" The most perfect coincidence. I smiled to myself, checking my phone to see if she'd texted back yet. "I'm going to grab a glass of wine. You want one?"

"Sure," Mom said. "Because I want to hear all about your new gal pal."

"Gal pal," I laughed. "Exactly."

I went inside and fed Stormy dinner, then poured two glasses of wine and walked back outside. Mom was looking at her phone. Her brow was furrowed.

"Bad news?" I asked.

She sighed, taking the wine. "Just your father, if you can believe that."

"He does have the impeccable skill of ruining a good moment," I said. I grabbed her phone and flipped it face down on the table. "There. Looks like you no longer have service."

Mom laughed, sipping the Chardonnay. "Oh, this is good. Okay, now tell me everything."

"Well, it was raining really hard," I began.

I recounted the past few whirlwind days. I'd gotten a girlfriend and a dog. It had been quite a weekend for my hermit tendencies, that was for sure.

Mom seemed sufficiently interested, but I could tell that she didn't think it was as serious as it was.

And it was serious. I had found Julia. I had gotten her back. And I would never make the mistake of losing her ever again.

CHAPTER FIFTEEN

Julia

Taco Bell wrappers cluttered the coffee table. Cameron sat on the other side, cross-legged, watching me tell her the full story all over again, but in person. She paused in the middle of a quesadilla bite, her eyes wide.

"A car?" She gasped. "No. You did *not* mention that."

"I'm obviously going to tell her I can't keep it," I said, scoffing. "But that doesn't mean I can't enjoy it for like, a few days."

"Yes, yeah, that's exactly what that means," Cameron said, shaking her head.

I lifted my shoulders. "So, that's basically everything."

"Don't you think this is all just slightly too good to be true?" She asked, leaning back against my television stand. She sipped loudly at her ridiculously bright Baja Blast soda that she had claimed was an essential part of any Taco Bell meal.

"What part?" I asked.

"What part?" She laughed, then realized I was serious. "I don't know, maybe the part where Remi lured you to her house, convinced you that your breakup was entirely externally motivated, and then became the perfect girlfriend seemingly overnight? Oh, and gave you an expensive-ass Volvo."

"Okay, I see the Baja Blast-colored lens you're viewing this through, but it's not like any of that," I said.

Cameron spoke slowly and clearly, as though it was purely a language barrier between us. "You think it was purely coincidence that her assistant hired you?"

I shrugged. "Yeah, I guess," I said. To be honest, I hadn't considered it that closely.

She nodded. "Sure. Sure sure sure. Okay. Next question, you honestly believe that she broke up with you because someone photoshopped photos of you cheating on her with..." She paused, gesturing as though she was flipping a page back and forth that she'd been reading. "Curtis?"

I took a deep breath. I knew it was her job as my best friend to be concerned for me, but this felt like a bit of an overstep. "Listen, I saw the pictures, I was there with her. I *know* she believed them."

Cameron nodded again, staring at me intensely. "Or maybe she's a really good actress."

Okay, that was enough. "Or maybe, you just have something against me being happy."

She rolled her eyes. "That was dramatic."

I wanted to slap the stupid green drink right out of her hand, but my rug was a cream color, and that shit would never come out of it. "So is believing that my girlfriend is part of a secret plot to ruin my life. For what gain, Cam?"

"I don't know," she said, looking upwards as though thinking about it. "Maybe she magically sensed that you had finally moved on."

I blinked slowly, staring at her. "Wow, had no idea you

were into spiritualism now, or maybe just stand-up comedy."

"Listen, I watched that breakup go down. If you remember correctly, I drove out to Denver and stayed with you for two weeks during that summer when you even getting dressed or showered was a huge ask. You used to hide in your closet and cry so I wouldn't see you."

"I did not." I lied.

"Here's what I didn't tell you," Cameron said, sitting up straighter and putting her drink down on the table with enough force to startle me. "I didn't tell you that Remington Van der Meer showed back up to campus looking completely normal. She didn't miss a beat. And when people asked her where you were, she barely even batted an eye. And then, that fucking woman showed up."

I blinked, taken aback by Cameron's intensity. "What woman?"

"Her new girlfriend. Alyssa or whatever."

"Wh-what? She came to McManus?"

"Yeah, it was like she came for a weekend and then never left. She and Remi were inseparable."

I tried to process the new information. Remi told me that they didn't get engaged until that summer, but that didn't mean they weren't together before. I felt light-headed, picturing Alison walking through McManus campus, which had always been gorgeous and bright and alive in spring.

"Are you sure they're even divorced?" Cameron raised her eyebrows at me.

My stomach lurched. Luckily, a quick online search showed that yes, they had gotten divorced. God bless public records.

I stood up, trying to wrap my head around everything. "Why can't you just be happy for me?"

Cameron stood, taking my hand in hers. "I am. I truly am. I just want you to be smart about this."

I pulled my hand out of hers and walked into my bedroom, closing the door behind me. I could worry, I could pace, I could believe everything Cameron had told me and twist a horrible story.

Or, I could do the adult thing and just ask Remi.

I dialed her number.

"Hey, Jude," she sang as she answered the phone.

"When did you and Alison start dating?" I asked, cutting straight to the point.

"Uh," Remi faltered. "Hold on really quick." And then, as if she was holding the phone away from her face for a moment, she told someone she'd be back. I assumed it was her mother, trying to squash the jealous feeling that it could be anyone but her mother. I was so paranoid after what Cameron had just said to me.

"Okay, sorry about that," she said. "Uh, I think we started dating right before graduation?"

"Did she come to McManus to see you?" I asked.

"Okay, hold on." She hung up the phone.

I stared down at the screen in shock for a moment until a video call notification came through.

"I'd rather have this talk face-to-face, but this is as close as we're going to get," she said, and I hated that she looked adorable. She was sitting on the edge of her bed. I could tell by the windows behind her.

"Did she come to McManus or not?" I asked.

Remi nodded, the video lagging slightly. "She came to visit right at the end, like maybe a week before graduation. And then she and her family helped me move out."

"Why did she help you move out?" I asked, feeling stupid even as the words came out of my mouth.

She looked confused. "Jude, I don't know what's going

on with these questions. Yes, she helped me move out. My dad didn't come to my graduation, and it wasn't like my mom was going to pack boxes with me," she said.

I sighed, frustrated with the situation and with myself. I sat down on the edge of my bed.

"Cameron said you didn't even seem upset when you came back to school." I pushed my hair out of my face, nervous and confused.

"Baby, Cameron and I weren't even good friends, so she only saw me in public, when I had time to put myself together between going to classes and studying for finals. What are you really trying to ask here?"

"Is this real?" The words came rushing out. I knew I was being insufferable and yet, I couldn't make myself stop.

"For me it is. I think you feel the same way, but if not, would you like to talk about it?" She almost looked hurt by the question.

I hated her when she was being so sensible and rational and calm.

"Was it purely a coincidence that your assistant hired me? Or did you set that up?" I asked.

Remi laughed, looking bewildered by the line of questioning. "I don't know if you remember how shocked I was to see you?"

I could picture her face as she opened the door, how her entire stance changed, how her eyes widened, how she stared at me like she wasn't sure I was real.

"I wish I could be there with you to have this talk in person," she said, shaking her head.

I wiped at my eyes hastily. "It's just that ten years is a long time. I'm worried that we're too late."

"I know there's a lot left that we need to iron out, but here's what you need to know for now, and of course I wish this was in person, but you need to hear it. I love you. I have always loved you, and never anyone else. I may have married Alison in a fit of weak resentment, but I've only loved you. Ever. I meant it when I asked you to make a life with me ten years ago, to let your future entwine with mine, and I still want that. I want nothing more than to have a future with you, whatever that looks like. We can take it slow, or we can elope tomorrow — I don't care. I just want to be with you."

A lump rose in my throat. I was unable to speak as tears fell down my cheeks.

"Okay?" She asked.

I nodded, laughing as I sniffled. "Yeah, I guess."

She grinned. "Cameron, I know you're listening at the door," she said, raising her voice.

Curious, I stood and opened the door to find my best friend standing there, awkwardly trying to look as though she hadn't just been leaning in to hear.

"Let me talk to her, Jude."

I handed the phone over to Cameron, a little nervous.

"H-hey Remington," she began, looking almost too uncomfortable to make eye contact.

"Listen, I'd be suspicious of me, too."

Cameron pressed her lips together and nodded.

"And I give you full permission to come for me with a shovel if I ever screw this up."

"Hey now," I started, laughing.

"I messed this up in college, but I'm trying to do it right this time. I promise," Remi said.

I leaned in to see the screen.

Cameron nodded. "I'm taking the murder agreement to heart."

"As you should." Remi said, nodding solemnly. "And I'm glad she has someone looking out for her."

Cameron smiled at that. "Always. She's the best, and I'm not letting anything happen to her."

"Me either." Remi smiled. "I should let you two get back to your Taco Bell."

My eyes widened in surprise. "How did you know?" I laughed.

"Some things never change," Remi said, winking. "Call me before bed? I have some news to tell you of the Stormy variety."

Excited, I nodded, and Cameron and I both waved as we hung up the call.

Cameron turned to me. "I really will kill her, though. Or at least take out her kneecaps."

"Alright, Tonya," I said, wrapping an arm around her shoulder as we walked back into my living room.

I CROSSED and uncrossed my legs nine thousand times under the table. My neighborhood cafe was noisy, but it was still cozy, and I needed a comfortable spot to meet others. Because I wasn't part of an agency, I mostly worked out of my home, and met clients and others at the cafe, instead.

Today, I had arranged three meetings with potential architectural partners for the afternoon, hoping that we could chat about collaborating on Remi's home. I'd brought my renderings, my ideas, the floor plans, everything. Because I was basically taking on the role of General Contractor, it was important that they viewed me as an authority, not just another subcontractor.

The first meeting had gone over... fine. Nothing about the guy really made me feel excited to work together. He was professional, but a little... bland. He had also corrected something I'd said — saying that the future floor plan probably wasn't that accurate, since I'd drawn it up myself.

What, so an interior designer couldn't understand AutoCAD? I was creative, not dumb.

The second person was running four minutes late, according to the last moment I'd checked my watch. I glanced at my wrist again. Okay, six minutes.

Fifteen minutes after our start time, a rumpled young man sat down at the table. "So sorry I'm late," he said. "I got lost."

"It happens. So, let's get right into it," I said, taking a deep breath.

"Wait, before we do, let me go grab a coffee," he interrupted.

I watched in disbelief as he stood, walked to the line, waited, ordered, and then waited at the counter for his drink. When he returned, I was taking deep, soothing breaths to prevent myself from yelling.

He sat, smiling at me. "Okay, let's talk about your little project." He took a sip of his coffee.

Little? This was a multi-year, major renovation I had in mind. Little was not the appropriate word.

He excused himself to grab a few packets of sugar from the condiment station, and returned.

"Okay, well—"

He began noisily stirring raw sugar into his coffee, the metal of the spoon slamming into the sides of the ceramic with shocking force.

I shut my laptop. "So nice meeting you. I think I'll be taking a different direction."

Fuck architects.

He was meant to be from a major firm that I respected. Why did they send the guy straight out of college, lacking in social skills? I couldn't wait to call them and let them know exactly why I would not be working with them now or in the future.

I stood, shoving my laptop into my bag, ready to bolt from the premises.

A woman in a blazer stood from a chair near the door as I started to leave. "I'm Quinn Koehler, your 3 o'clock. I got here a bit early, so I figured I'd wait out of your way. You're not leaving, are you?"

I paused, mortified. "Oh, I'm so sorry. I just..." I hooked a thumb over my shoulder at the guy who was now noisily blowing his nose in a tissue.

"Oof, yeah, I can't blame you. Want to chat outside?" She asked, reaching for the door to hold it for me.

Quinn was in her late 40s or early 50s with short dark hair, graying at the temples. She was wearing men's slacks and sensible shoes. I tried not to let my blatant favoritism for a perhaps-queer woman take over my mind.

She sat in a seat across from me, adjusting the umbrella above our table to shield us from the sun. "Okay, much better. Now, about this project. I'm so excited to potentially work with you. The plans your office sent over make it look like a genuinely interesting reno."

I smiled, taken aback by her intensity and sincerity.

She pulled a laptop out of her bag, taking glasses and putting them on as she smiled across the table at me. "Alright, tell me everything."

I described the house, how it was nice enough, but could really be elevated with a few changes. I opened my own laptop, flipping through photos to describe the basis behind my ideas.

"I'm nervous about this wall removal," she said, pointing to the floor plan we'd just unrolled. "With that placement, I'd bet anything it's structural." She bit her lip. "Without seeing the property in person, I'm only guessing, of course, but there are ways we can work around that. We could enclose the support in a pillar, we could try to shift the placement by six feet, we could alter the design just slightly to include part of this wall, but remove this one here, instead..." She pointed to the drawing.

I agreed with her, growing more excited as she threw out ideas that complimented my own, adding in examples that I'd never considered.

I found myself nodding and smiling, agreeing with her because I wanted to, not because I felt pressured to.

"I'd love to see the property in person. Is there a good time this week or next that I could meet you up there?"

We formulated a plan to see the house on the following Monday, which worked out perfectly since I was missing Remi miserably and wanted an excuse to see her again.

My car had already been towed, but I hadn't needed to be there for the insurance adjustment. Sure enough, they'd totalled my car and written me a check for about what I owed for it, which wasn't saying much.

Cameron was staying with me through the weekend and would be there during the beginning of the next week, and it was comforting to have her with me, sitting beside me on the couch as we worked or watched Parks and Rec in our work "breaks." It was just like college. It was funny, I was so different from who I was then, but with Remi back in my life and Cameron sleeping on my couch, it felt a lot like it always had.

And I would have minded that a few months ago, but not now. Now? I was still anticipatory, but full of hope.

CHAPTER SIXTEEN

REMINGTON

I STARED DOWN AT THE CALLER ID. IT WAS MY FATHER.

And I had been having such a lovely afternoon, too. Mom and I had taken a walk with Stormy, and we'd visited Flossie and checked in on her — she had even convinced my mother to have some Long Island Iced Teas on the patio while Stormy and I drank Topo Chicos.

And now, Diederik was calling to ruin it all.

I glanced toward where Mom was sitting with Flossie around a fire pit. Mom hated campfires, but she looked perfectly content next to Flossie. That woman sure could charm the pants off anyone — well, excluding me.

I walked through the house and stepped out the front door, taking the call as I sat down on the first step.

"This is Remington," I said, knowing the formality would piss him off.

"Well, hello, Mrs. Van der Meer," he said. He almost sounded cheerful? My hackles raised at that.

"It's Ms. now. You should know that better than anyone. Is something horribly wrong?" I asked.

He cleared his throat. "You know why I'm calling."

Had he heard about Julia?

"Why did you fire your assistant?" He asked.

What? "I'd never fire Kelly. I need Kelly." What I meant was, I'd sooner chop out my own liver than do anything to Kelly.

"Hmm." He sounded deeply skeptical. "Well, she packed up her desk."

"I'm on my way," I said, standing from the front porch. "Who gave the order?"

"Everyone thought it was from you," he said.

"Are you fucking with me?" I asked, my professional mask falling as my heart began to race.

"Honestly? I wish I was," he said. "But no. I can look into it, if you'd like."

"No, I can look into this myself, since it was supposedly me who did the firing." There had to be some kind of paper trail.

"While we're on the subject of leaving the company," he said casually.

"Excuse me?" My jaw had already dropped.

He sighed. "A little birdy told me you were exploring your options."

"Was it the same birdy that told you to fire Kelly?" I set my jaw, fisting and unfisting my hand.

"Honestly, Remington. That wasn't me." He cleared his throat. "I simply heard you're considering other positions."

I decided not to answer that directly and sighed.

"I think it's an intelligent move," he said, catching me off guard. What was his angle here?

"Oh, do you?" I was unable to think of a better, catchier response.

"I do, Remington. Honestly. I know you've been unhappy here for awhile," he said.

"Yeah, well, you've kind of made a working relationship difficult for a number of reasons." I took a deep breath, trying to remain cool and calm. He always loved it when I lost my temper, because it meant that he'd won. Not today.

"I understand your frustration."

I wanted to throw something, hearing that. He understood my frustration?! First, he sabotaged my one shot at real happiness by convincing Julia and me that we had both been unfaithful to each other, and then he had an affair with my wife, and now he wanted to say he understood?

"Well, I'm glad I have your blessing to leave," I said through clenched teeth.

"Just one thing," he said with forced casualty.

"Hmm?" I rubbed the bridge of my nose.

He lowered his voice. "Don't trust your mother. I know she's there with you, but don't trust her."

"Darling, who are you talking to?" Mom interrupted me.

I jumped at the sound of her voice. "Diederik," I said.

She looked annoyed instantly at the mention of her husband's name. And everyone wondered why I'd stayed in a loveless marriage for so long. With role models like these, how would I have ever known anyone had a real shot at being happy?

"Oh, is that Emily? Send her my regards."

What I wanted to say: Fuck right off with that.

What I said: "Sure."

I gave my own regards to my father, hanging up the phone.

Mom tilted her head, looking at me curiously. "How was your chat?"

I shrugged, kicking the toe of my boot at the ground.

"What did he want?"

"The usual. Just to torment me forever, I suppose." I really didn't feel like rehashing it.

"What did he say?" She asked.

"If you're so interested, why don't you just call him yourself?" I snapped, then immediately felt guilty for snapping at my own mother.

She blinked, watching me.

What had he meant by not trusting her? Was he just trying to get in my head?

"Fuck, I have to call Kelly and tell her she's not fired," I said, reaching for my phone.

Mom touched my arm. "Let's walk home first. Whatever it is, everything will work out fine, I'm sure."

How was she so sure? I grabbed Stormy's leash and found her snoozing on a rug in Flossie's hallway.

Flossie appeared in the doorway. "Everything okay, kiddo?" She asked.

"Not really," I grumbled.

"Want to talk about it?" She offered.

I shook my head. "Dads," I shrugged.

"You know, I'm alright with the idea that people may think I'm a bonkers hermit, living alone up here," she said, leaning against the wall, watching me with interest.

I waited for her to continue, but she was just watching me.

"So?" I said, impatient.

"I've made my own happiness." She smiled, adjusting one of the silver and turquoise bangles around her wrist.

"What's the secret to that?" I asked.

She gestured me forward, like she was about to tell me a real secret. I took the bait, leaning in slightly.

"Never giving a fuck what anyone thought, especially my family. Buncha rat bastards, if you ask me." She laughed.

I stared at her in confusion.

Flossie sighed. "I don't know why Julia likes you, but she does, so I'll continue to tolerate you for her sake, because she's something special. But I tell you, you'll walk easier without that giant stick up your ass."

I did grin at that.

"Oh, I promised her I'd give her something," she said, turning to walk out of the room.

Mom poked her head back in the door. "Are you almost ready?"

I nodded, turning as Flossie reappeared with what seemed like a roll of wallpaper tucked under an arm. She handed it to me. I made a move to open it, but she quickly shook her head. "It's precious stuff, don't rip it. Leave that stuff to the professionals, dearie."

Weird, but everything about Flossie was weird. It seemed to be kind of her thing. I said my goodbyes and walked out with Stormy.

GOOD LORD, I was tired of calling people. I moved to the mountains in a remote location to be away from people, not more connected than I'd ever been before.

"VDM?" Kelly asked as she answered the phone. She sounded sniffly, like she'd been crying. I'd only seen her cry twice in our professional relationship. Once when her granddaughter was born and once when David Bowie died. In fact, I'd been so disconcerted by her response to the latter that I'd given her bereavement time.

"Kelly, you're not fired," I said as fast as I could.

"I'm not?" She sniffled again.

"Why would I ever fire you?" I asked.

She took in a deep, shaky breath. "I don't know. I thought it might have something to do with you leaving or maybe those files."

I wasn't following. "The files? Because I made you scan them in?"

"No, because of how I had them," she said, clearing her throat.

That didn't sound good. "What do you mean, *how you had them?*"

She paused.

"Tell me as a friend, not a boss," I said calmly, trying to unravel the story.

"Is your mother still visiting?" She asked.

Nice try on the change of subject.

"I wasn't changing the subject," she quickly said.

How was she doing that even in this tense moment?

"Remington, listen to me. I have something important that you need to know, but I need to tell you in person. Can you come to Chicago?"

I glanced at the calendar. I had the meeting with the board at Guardian in two days. "Can I fly you into Denver instead?"

She cleared her throat. "Sure. As long as you meet me alone."

"Any reason why you're being Mafia-levels of cryptic?" I asked.

She finally did chuckle at that. "I think you'll understand exactly why when I tell you."

Wow, I hated that. I sighed. "Well, you're not fired. Buy a ticket to Denver — Monday sounds like it would work, but I can make anything work. I'm so sorry you've had to go through this."

She made a quiet mmhmm sound.

"I mean it, Kelly. You're important to me and I need you."

She let out a quiet gasp, sounding startled. "Well, thank you."

We said our goodbyes and she sent an itinerary to my personal email address, not my work email. Weird. She'd be in town starting the day after tomorrow, Monday. Maybe I'd travel down to Julia's later tomorrow and stay a few nights.

I texted Julia.

Me: Does your apartment allow dogs?

Julia: Sure does. But why?

Me: Can I crash at yours for a few days?

Julia: Yeah, but Cameron is in the second bedroom, so you'll have to stay on the couch.

Me: I know you live in a one bedroom, liar.

Julia: Fine, see you soon.

I stood, stretching. It had been a long day between talking to my dad and then smoothing things over with Kelly. What a nightmare.

I walked into the living room where Mom sat with a book. "Alright, I have to go down to Denver for that interview. I was thinking of going tomorrow to save myself the trouble of traveling the morning of. Did you want to stay here alone or do you want to leave a day early?"

She set her book down, looking annoyed. "Oh, our visit is going to end a little early? But I thought we were having a good time."

"I know, it's just—"

"And we so rarely ever get to see each other," she

started. My mother was a serious professional with guilt trips.

"I know, but—"

"I mean, I know your new interview is important. I just don't see why they aren't a little more flexible to your schedule."

"I'm the one who said I'd be there on Monday," I said. "So, this shouldn't be coming out of nowhere."

She nodded, her expression changing to disappointment. She took a deep breath and let it out slowly in the world's longest sigh.

"Think about it. We still have another day. You're more than welcome to stay here. I just think you might be bored. Or you could always call up Flossie to hang out," I joked.

"She's such a peculiar woman," she said, squinting in thought. "Normally I don't let people like that talk to me much, but she was amusing for a while."

"People like what?" I asked.

"You know what I mean, darling."

Why did I suddenly feel defensive about Flossie? "No, I don't suppose I do," I said, crossing my arms.

She rolled her eyes. "Alright, well, I'll pack up my things tonight, then. But if it's too much of a hassle for you to drive me to the airport, I can get a cab."

"I can drive you."

"It just doesn't seem like you want to spend much time with me and it's such a long drive."

The drive was only about two and a half hours in good traffic, and now that they'd cleared up the road between Breckenridge and the interstate, it would be a relatively quick trip. I took a deep, cleansing, patience-enhancing breath. "It is not a problem for me to drive you," I said.

She pressed her lips into a thin line. "Okay, well, if you insist."

She waited until I was preparing dinner, sliding onto a barstool to look at me across the kitchen island. She was watching me, and I grew more uncomfortable as she continued to do so without talking.

"Hey, you okay?" I asked, trying to break the icy silence.

"You know, I always thought you might get back together with Alison." Her voice was incredibly nonchalant.

"Excuse me?" I chopped a little too hard through the cauliflower head on the cutting board. It crumbled, sending florets in various directions.

"Every couple has their ups and downs, darling."

"She cheated on me." I sputtered. "With *Dad*."

Mom shrugged.

"That doesn't alarm you in any way?" I asked, incredulous. "You *hate* your husband."

"Everyone has secrets and things they'd rather forget about. You just work through them, honey," she said.

"That's terrible advice," I argued.

"Remember when you first started dating her, and I explained that marriage is a business partnership?" She asked.

"Also terrible advice." I put the knife down on the counter, turning to face her as I wiped my hands on my apron. "Your marriage is a business partnership. That doesn't mean all marriages should be."

"Just promise me you won't marry this girl," she said, her mouth pressing together firmly.

I stared at her, nearly speechless. "What girl? Julia? She's a 32-year-old woman, Mom. And we've been dating for like, four days, so the wedding invites aren't ordered just yet. Give me a week, at least."

"I'm just worried that you're going to throw your

entire life away on this false notion of happiness and love," she continued, her voice steady and calm.

I took a deep breath. It was important to me that she understood I was serious. "Well, I love her, and she makes me happy, and that's enough for me. I don't need anything else." I stared her down, daring her to argue with that.

"You always do this, Remington. You're a naive optimist and you jump right into things. I've spent the last twenty years trying to keep you from this reckless behavior, and it hurts me to see you do it again and again. This woman, the dog, this new job. You jump in head first without looking."

She narrowed her eyes, but didn't say anything.

"I don't need you to keep me from being reckless. I don't even need you to patch it up when I am hurt. I need you to take ten steps back and let me live my own life for once." I felt like an angry teenager, but this is precisely the type of conversation she'd never allowed us to have when I was younger.

"I refuse to be a part of it," she said, holding up her palms as though she was surrendering.

The drama was incredible. Someone get the woman an Oscar.

She left the room, then returned with her suitcase. "It's clear that you don't want me here."

A familiar pang of guilt stabbed me. "That's not true, Mom."

"I've called a cab," she said. "I'm taking the shuttle to the airport."

I almost laughed at the mental image of her taking public transportation with her designer suitcase.

"Travel safe," I said, turning my back.

I heard the door open and shut, and I laid my palms on the cold granite of the countertop, blinking back tears.

I skipped dinner, putting the ingredients back into containers and shoving them in the fridge.

I sat in the living room, basking in the aloneness as I listened to records, staring at the cabinet Julia had painted. Such a simple change, and yet it had such an impact. I felt proud of her, and even more than that, excited to grow together, excited to learn more about the way her brain worked now.

Yes, I was jumping in head first, but what a thrilling feeling it was.

I AWOKE to a phone call and squinted, seeing Nick's name on the screen. I answered, rolling onto my side to hug Stormy, who had taken over the other half of my bed sometime in the night.

"Good morning," I said. "How are you?"

"She's hesitant, but she knows it's the right decision," Nick said.

"What?" It was too early for him to be vague.

"You can adopt Kiki if you'd like," he said, speaking slowly and using my own vocabulary back to me. I was sure that if I hadn't used that specific word, he'd have said to keep her, like she was some kind of object to be passed around.

I sat straight up in bed, smiling. Relief washed over me, releasing a tension that I didn't realize I was holding. "Thank you, I really appreciate that. And tell your daughter that she can call anytime."

Nick snorted. "You bet. Take good care of her."

I hung up with him, looking down at Stormy, who had rolled onto her back to beg for belly rubs. "Oh, you poor neglected soul. Never getting belly rubs in your life." Her face split into a smile, and I wrapped my arms around her.

"You picked me, and I promise to be a really good mom. And Julia is going to be a really good mom, too, but I can be your favorite mom, okay?"

Her tail wagged. I took that as an agreement.

The car ride into the city was relatively uneventful. I chose the SUV instead of the Jeep to keep Stormy comfortable on the interstate. She sat in the backseat, staring out the window with interest. I wondered how often she'd been in a car before meeting me. She wasn't badly behaved, but she was curious and acting like everything was brand new to her. It made me smile to catch her dopey grin in the rearview mirror.

I pulled into Julia's apartment, which was built into an old house in the middle of the city. It was everything I hated, and yet, when I walked through the door, I felt home at once. Mostly because she was there, wrapping her arms around me and kissing me hello, but also because she had impeccable design sense, making the small space seem large and stylish.

I was relieved once again that she'd returned to me. After the cruel argument with my mother, Julia's presence was a balm.

As Julia loved on Stormy, I turned to Cameron. She seemed shy to say hello to me and tried to reach out a hand to shake mine, but I pulled her in for a hug anyway. She gasped in surprise but hugged me tightly nonetheless.

"Good to see you again," I said to her, and I genuinely meant it.

"I was just schooling Cameron in dominoes. You want to join?" Julia asked, taking my hand.

As we fell asleep, basking in the familiar giddiness after trying to have quiet sex that Cameron wouldn't hear, I knew that Julia was my true North. I was better because of her. Braver, more confident.

I had the sense that the following few days would just continue to get stranger. Kelly's words echoed in my mind. What could she possibly have to tell me that was so important, so scary, that she couldn't even say it over the phone?

CHAPTER SEVENTEEN

JULIA

"Oh my god, this road is awful," Cameron said, shifting in the backseat to be located directly in the middle as she held onto the front headrests. Stormy welcomed the invasion into her personal space with a lick to Cameron's cheek.

"Yeah, try it in the rain, Evel Knieval," I joked.

To be honest, I was still white knuckling the steering wheel as I continued up the steep dirt road with a trillion foot drop-off to the right edge. How did anyone navigate this treacherous terrain in winter?

"It is kind of alarming," Quinn admitted, holding the handle over the passenger side window. She looked a little green around the gills.

"We're almost there, I promise," I said, watching for the Peak 8 Ranch sign. As I came around a curve, a massive truck driving at an erratic speed came around the turn and I gasped.

"Our Father, who art in Heaven, hallowed be thy name," Cameron whispered from the backseat.

I'd recognize that ridiculous old truck — Big Bertha — anywhere. Flossie slowed to a near-complete stop once I rolled down my window and waved. She paused and smiled widely at me. She had on a cut-off muscle tee that showed off her tattoos.

"Hey, I didn't know you were paying us a visit so soon," she said, leaning out her window.

"This is the architect for Remi's renovation," I said, gesturing to the passenger seat.

Flossie pushed her oversized sunglasses onto her head. "Well, hello there. Welcome to the neighborhood."

Quinn blinked in confusion.

"And that's my best friend." I said, pointing over my shoulder.

"Tell me you're not referring to the dog as your best friend." Flossie waved toward the back window and I glanced over my shoulder to find that Stormy had pushed her head through the small opening, panting and wiggling at the sight of Flossie.

"I'll pop by after I get back from town." Flossie said.

I nodded and we continued on the road.

"I love her," Cameron said.

"Me too," I said with a laugh. I pulled into Remi's driveway, thankful that the small bridge had been repaired in my absence.

It was strange to be back at her mansion without her. She was still in Denver for her big Board meeting, and was staying at my place for one more night while I was up here. We'd made good time during the off-time on a Monday afternoon, but I figured we'd be staying the night given the hour. I'd already booked Quinn a room in town, but Stormy, Cameron, and I were going to sleep at the house.

As the trees thinned and the house came into view, my

heart sped up. It truly was a gorgeous place. All long lines and bold statements. It didn't quite fit into the environment, but it was still a gorgeous building with a breathtaking view. It was confident and unapologetic in its beauty. It reminded me a lot of Remi in that way.

We hopped out of the car and I unlocked the front door using the door code she'd given me. I tapped in the alarm code and walked into the kitchen, opening the fridge to grab a La Croix after the long drive.

"Wow, you seem pretty at home here," Cameron commented, walking into the kitchen with her neck craned as she looked around. I offered her and Quinn drinks. Cameron agreed to a diet soda, but Quinn said she was fine without anything just yet.

Stormy ran immediately to where I assumed Remi was keeping her food. I opened the cupboard to find her bowl and filled it for her. It was almost dinnertime anyway.

Quinn was taking pictures and typing furiously into her phone. When she glanced up to see me watching her, she blushed. "Sorry, already taking notes," she said. "You were right, this place is great, but it could be fantastic with a few minor adjustments."

I walked back out to the car to grab my bag and the original floor plans, as well as the ideas we'd come up with the other day at the cafe. Quinn had already sent me a third version to consider, and I agreed with almost all of her shifts. She had a good eye, and I felt respected by the changes she'd made.

I pushed the door closed behind me with my foot, my arms too full of design goodness to bother with resetting the alarm. Whatever, who was going to break in — the homicidal chipmunks?

We walked around as I gave her my spiel. She already had a structural engineer lined up to take a look at a few areas that may prove problematic, but overall, we agreed on what needed to happen. The process was alarmingly fast for how large the place was — though, to be fair, it wasn't like we were tearing out an entire section of the house.

The kitchen would prove to be a little interesting, since my idea was to shift where the sink and oven were, so there would be some rewiring and rerouting of pipes, but Quinn said it was a good idea, which warmed my heart a bit.

Cameron opened the patio door and walked outside to take in the view of the forested valley below.

Quinn had already suggested changing the entire row of glass panes to a type of door that could completely fold and slide into the wall, opening the space up entirely. Given how much I knew Remi loved to sit on the back porch, I loved the idea.

"You really have an eye for this," I said, following her outside. She wanted a look at the building from the back to make sure we weren't missing something.

"I'm really excited about this project," she admitted, looking a little bashful to be saying so. "You know, I originally went to school for interior design, and shifted my focus to architecture only for an advanced degree. You remind me of the excitement I once had for it."

I stared at her in surprise. "Wow, that's really kind of you to say."

"You know, I'm bidding on an upcoming project and I'd love to get your thoughts on collaborating on architecture and design," she said over her shoulder as I followed her down the patio stairs. "It's for a small hotel in Santa Fe."

"Yes!" I exclaimed way too quickly and loudly. "I mean, sure, absolutely, that sounds really interesting."

She smiled. "I'll have my assistant send things over to your office."

So flattering that she thought I had an office.

I nodded, beaming, bouncing down the rest of the stairs.

We stood near the tree line and talked about the massive three-story windows, weighing the pros and cons of suggesting future renovation ideas for limiting the amount of distracting framing that was just a bit too thick to be invisible. It was less obvious from inside, but the idea of it being almost seamless was too tempting. Hmm, I'd check with Remi on the budget.

The air was fresh — it was still hot in that tiring end-of-summer way, where I was ready for fall, but the world wasn't just quite there yet. I twisted my hair up into a bun to keep it off of my neck and out of my way. I hadn't been straightening it lately, and the curl-frizz-in-heat was driving me to frustration. The trees hadn't even started changing colors. I couldn't wait to sit on the deck and watch as they did.

Butterflies swirled in my stomach as I pictured being here for the fall and winter, cozying in during snowstorms. Maybe those storms wouldn't knock out the power like the rains had.

"Alright, let's take a seat at the table and brainstorm a bit more concretely?" Quinn suggested, heading back up to the house.

Cameron stood at the railing. "Hey Julia, I think your friend is here," she called down.

I checked my watch. We'd only been there for just over an hour. Flossie had been quick on her trip. Sure enough, the older woman's head peeked over the railing, complete with the furry trapper hat I'd met her in. "Get your ass up here, I'm making margaritas."

Quinn laughed good-naturedly. "Why do I have the feeling these plans are going to get very interesting if we have a few of these margaritas?"

"Hope you like jalapenos!" Flossie added, cupping her hands around her mouth to make her voice carry.

Uh oh.

Two jalapeno margaritas later, the four of us were sitting in the great room while Stormy slept on the kitchen rug, most likely hoping I'd forgotten that I'd already fed her dinner.

Quinn was such a good sport — she'd been the one to suggest we take a break and give into Flossie's plan to make us relax a bit.

Quinn had just finished telling us about the last project she'd worked on — a boring and lifeless corporate high rise that had inspired her to try something smaller and more interesting. Hence, the Van der Meer residence.

"Wow, smart *and* beautiful," Flossie said to Quinn, giving her a confident smile.

Shameless.

Quinn blushed, giving her a shy smile in return.

I reached to lightly touch Cameron's arm without looking at her, our silent signal for 'We're absolutely going to talk about this later.'

I caught her subtle nod in return.

It felt so different to be here without Remi — I still couldn't wait to get the woman a different couch, complete with comfortable sitting chairs. As it was, Cameron and I were sitting in chairs we'd pulled in from the dining room and let Quinn and Flossie take the couch.

So much had happened in the past... what was it, just over one week? The entire course of my life had changed. It was a lot to deal with, and yet, when I was with Remi, I was sure that every choice we were making was right. It just felt different with her. Everything seemed to click into place now that she was in my life.

I texted her to ask her how meeting the Board had gone. I knew she was meeting her assistant that evening, but she'd been a bit tight-lipped about why her assistant was suddenly flying in. I wondered if she'd be staying for a few days, and if I'd get to meet her after talking to her on the phone in the conversation that started this entire roller-coaster ride.

Remi: Baby, it went so well. Obviously they have to have an official meeting about it, and there's a few more things to iron out, but I have a good feeling. Two of them even privately told me it was clear I was a perfect fit.

Me: Yay! So proud of you! Madame CEO.

Remi: Don't you jinx me.

"Someone's in love," Cameron sing-songed as she looked at me.

I found myself smiling down at my phone. "Nuh uh," I said.

Flossie raised a brow at me. "I've always thought that you should fall in love as often and as quickly as possible."

Quinn pushed her hair out of her face with her fingers, idly playing with a strand. "How many times have you been married?" She asked coyly.

"Four." Flossie was confident and proud of her number.

Quinn laughed. "I see you've followed your own advice."

"What's the point of giving out extremely valuable advice if you don't intend to follow it yourself?" Flossie said, raising her eyebrows.

Quinn laughed again.

I got a new text notification and checked my phone.

Cameron: GET THESE TWO A ROOM

Me: (heart eyes emoji) (green nausea emoji)

Cameron chuckled under her breath beside me.

"I'm hungry, what's for dinner?" Cameron asked, turning towards me innocently.

I grimaced. "I hadn't thought that far in advance," I admitted. I stood, walking into the kitchen. I opened the pantry, finding a few boxes of mac and cheese — wow, Remi was really leaning into that bachelor life. We'd mostly subsisted off of easy, quick meals during my time here the week before. I opened the freezer to see if she had any more frozen veggies I could toss in the microwave.

"I can help," Cameron said from behind me. She opened the pantry. "Orzo. Ooh, and look at this fancy apron." She pulled out a piece of fabric and popped it over her head, tying it around her waist. It was a flowery print and said, "Kiss the cook."

"Remi would sooner die," I said, laughing. I snapped a picture and texted it to her.

I heard the door open and shut, and I glanced back to the great room. Flossie and Quinn were talking closely on the couch. Cameron was right beside me. Stormy sat up, staring towards the front of the house. Her hackles raised as she stood, pinning her ears back.

Cameron looked down at her, confused. "What the—"

I grabbed a kitchen knife from the ugly knife block on the counter and took a step in the direction of the front door.

Stormy growled.

A tall, slim woman stepped into the light of the great room, looking at me with annoyance and confusion. She held a designer bag under her arm and her hair was perfectly coiffed into a sleek low pony that looked irritatingly chic.

"Who the hell are you?" I asked.

"Alison?" Cameron said, sounding shocked.

My blood turned ice cold and my chest clenched. I hardly recognized her from her social media account, but now that I was looking at her, it was clear. She had ashy blonde hair and perfectly contoured cheeks. Her eyebrows looked a lot better now than they had looked on Facebook ten years ago.

I reached for Stormy's collar, afraid she'd pick up on my mood and maul Remi's ex-wife to death before I could stab her instead.

"Where's Remington?" Alison said, looking around.

Flossie appeared by my side. "Do I need to go get my gun?" She asked, hooking her thumbs into the belt loops of her high-waisted jeans.

"What? No. This is Remi's ex-wife."

"Yeah, I'll go get the gun, then." Flossie said, walking out of the room before I could stop her.

Alison glanced at the large chef's knife in my hand, then back to my face with boredom.

I set the knife back in its place. "You have thirty seconds to tell me what you're doing here before I either release the hounds or Flossie."

She yawned, looking around curiously. "You know, it's funny, but I've never even been here."

Cameron crossed her arms over her chest. "Probably for good reason."

I grabbed my phone and called Remi. She picked up on the second ring. "Hey babe, I can't really talk right now," she said quickly. She sounded out of breath. "Everything okay?"

"No. Everything okay with you?" I was a bit alarmed by her tone. Why did Remi sound like she'd just had the wind knocked out of her?

"No." Her voice was soft, like she was having a hard time admitting that.

I cleared my throat, fidgeting with my hair. "Alison's here."

"Excuse me?"

I took a deep breath, turning my back on Alison. "You heard right. So, I could really use your help."

"Fuck. Okay. I'll be there in..." She paused, presumably looking at her watch. "Less than three hours. Feel free to kick her out."

I turned to see Alison watching me, her heel tapping on the hardwood floor.

"She's on her way." I said.

"Perfect." She said, smiling to show her perfect white teeth, the expression not even touching her eyes.

CHAPTER EIGHTEEN

REMINGTON

I WALKED DOWN THE STREET FEELING LIGHTER THAN AIR. THE
entire day of meetings and interviews had gone even
better than I'd planned — I'd impressed the Board, but
most importantly I'd make a solid impression on Steven,
the Chair of the Board. He had invited me to grab a drink
with him after the day had finished, and told me over an
Old Fashioned that I'd secured his vote.

Was it terrible that I wanted to call my father and brag?

I checked my watch for the time again. I was about five
minutes late to meeting with Kelly, who had told me to
meet her at some bar in LoDo. I considered hopping on
one of the free buses to get there faster, but instead just
sped up, my shoes uncomfortably stiff as I tried to walk as
fast as I could.

I opened the door to the bar and found that it was
fairly packed. There, in a back corner, Kelly sat with a fizzy
drink in her hand. She had a suitcase at her side. Why
hadn't she taken my advice and checked in to her hotel
until I could get there?

I reached her, a little breathless, and touched her shoulder as I stepped up to the table. It felt like ages since I'd seen her. I'd missed her more than I'd realized.

I hugged her as she stood, and she stayed still for a moment, as if surprised by the gesture. Surely we'd hugged before, right? I couldn't remember.

"You're in a good mood," she said as we sat down at the table.

"Will you go to Guardian with me?" I asked.

She blinked. "That's a little presumptuous. You don't even know if you're being offered the job. Don't you have a few more rounds to go?"

I nodded. I was absolutely getting a little ahead of myself. "Just say if I do, you'll come with me."

She closed one eye, wrinkling her nose as though she was thinking hard about it. "Okay."

"Really?" My voice was slightly too loud. I was a little excited.

She looked at me like I'd grown a second head.

"Listen, Kelly, I'd never fire you. In fact, you're way more likely to fire *me*. I need you," I said. Wow, I felt like I was grovelling, but she deserved it.

She nodded, blinking, then waved a server over. "Ice water, please. An entire pitcher. No straw. Also do you have tea? She'll have an herbal tea."

"But I want a straw with the water." I didn't even like tea.

She reached into her purse, pulling a metal straw out of a pouch.

"That's extremely forward-thinking of you," I said, turning the straw over in my hands.

"Okay, now, what I'm actually here to discuss," she said, taking a deep breath. She waited until the server left the table again, then looked around.

"Seriously, are we accidentally in the mafia or what?" I asked, looking around, too.

She rolled her eyes. "Remington, you have to believe me when I say that I found this entirely by accident." She reached into the bag at her side and pulled out a file folder. "Spring 2010" was written on the label in familiar handwriting.

"What's this?" I asked, opening the folder carefully. Inside were all of the original photos taken of Julia, then photos taken where the woman was clearly not Julia, then photoshopped and printed versions where the woman was made to look more like her. It was so obvious to me now, how could I have been so blind? "Yeah, Kelly, I know about this. I had you scan them in."

Kelly cleared her throat. "Just, keep looking."

I got past the photos to the text messages and the phone logs. "Yeah, these too," I said, flipping through them. I looked up to her. "What are you trying to tell me?"

She lifted her chin toward the folder. "Just keep going."

Falling somewhere between curious about what she was trying to tell me and irritated at the pictures I'd looked through, I continued. Past the phone logs were copies of checks made out to Curtis. Wow, most obvious paper trail in the world. Then, a contract with Curtis. I cringed, reading through the NDA-esque wording.

Kelly leaned over, pointing to the bottom of the contract. The signature. Beside Curtis Bass's last name was my mother's signature.

Wait... what?

I flipped back to the checks. They'd been signed by her.

What in the world? I looked up at Kelly. "So, this means that..."

She nodded. "It was your mother who set the whole thing up, not your father."

I felt as though the floor had dropped out from under me. My mother? Emily Van der Meer? Mom? Why did that make so much sense? Why did flames suddenly burst onto the sides of my face at the realization?

"How long have you known about this?" I took a sip of the tea that I was grateful she'd ordered me. My head was pounding and my entire body had goosebumps. It was so planned, so calculated. So evil.

"I found it last month," she said, shifting in her seat uncomfortably. "You asked me to grab a file out of your father's office, and I found it then."

"Last month?" I repeated, shocked. "And you didn't come to me immediately?"

"I didn't know if you were in a place to hear it yet."

"Wait a second. If you knew about it last month, that means that you hired Julia on purpose. That was no coincidence."

"I did some internet sleuthing, I'll admit."

I stared at her. "I can't believe you just..." I was unable to even say it aloud. It was both a favor and a massive overstep of boundaries.

"You're not through it all yet, VDM," she said, frowning.

I shut the file, unable to look through any more. "Give me the Cliff Notes version."

"Your mother hand-picked Alison to be your wife. She had already made an arrangement with the Dawes family. I'm not sure what part Alison played in it, but it was no coincidence that she showed back up in your life right at the same time. Then, and here's where I'm slightly confused, there's a contract with Alison."

"Like a prenup? But without my consent?" I asked. When would the supposed calming effects of this tea kick in? Any moment now?

My phone rang, and I glanced down at the screen for the first time since sitting down with Kelly. It was Julia. "Apologies. Hold on," I said, picking up the phone. "Hey babe, I can't really talk right now." Kelly was flipping through the pages on the table again. "Everything okay?"

"No. Everything okay with you?" Julia sounded panicked, her voice wavering like it usually did right before she burst into tears.

"No." I said, worried about her answer.

She cleared my throat. "Alison's here."

"Excuse me?" I looked up at Kelly, mouthing the words that Alison had shown up at the house.

"You heard right. So, I could really use your help." This was the last thing that I wanted to happen to Julia. I wanted to be a constant for her, stable in all ways so that she'd never have to worry about my intentions. She'd never have to worry about me breaking her heart ever again.

"Fuck. Okay. I'll be there in..." I glanced at my watch. "Less than three hours. Feel free to kick her out."

We hung up and I took a deep breath. "Well, want to see the cabin?" There was no way I was letting Crafty Kelly out of my sight.

She grimaced. "Is it snowing there?"

"It's August, Kelly," I said, tossing a few bills onto the table and standing. I grabbed the handle of Kelly's suitcase. "No snow."

We wound our way out of the bar. "Oh, just torrential rains, then?"

"Nah, we got that out of our system before you came, don't worry." I joked as we hit the street. I called a rideshare to take us to the garage where I'd parked the car that morning.

"So, why do you think Alison is at the cabin?" She asked.

I shrugged. "Maybe it has something to do with what's in the contract."

She chewed on her lip in thought. "Maybe, actually."

We made solid time on the drive up into the mountains. Kelly had only panicked twice, once during a steep descent in grade that I had maybe taken slightly too fast, and once in the Eisenhower Tunnel, but only because she swore she saw the roof leaking and was convinced the entire mountain would crumble down on us.

I thought a lot about why Kelly would overstep like that, instead of just coming to me with the files. She obviously wasn't in my life then and hadn't ever seen me with Julia, but she knew I was miserable. She was there for me during my divorce. She was practically my best friend... which was a rather stunning realization, actually.

She read me the contract with Alison, and she was right — something was missing. She pointed out that it was a copy in poor quality, so perhaps something had gotten lost or was hidden in the copying process? I guess I could ask Alison myself in just a few more minutes.

I drove through town, turning onto the main winding road that led to the steeper dirt road. I noticed Kelly holding the door tightly, but she didn't outright panic à la tunnel.

I knew we didn't have much time left to talk just the two of us. We'd be to the house in less than fifteen minutes, but my anger was still bubbling up inside me, and I knew I'd explode if I didn't vent it out now.

"I just don't understand why you weren't honest with me," I said.

"I know I overstepped," she said.

"You did." I nodded, pressing my lips into a thin line to avoid saying anything worse.

"You know how sometimes you act like I can read your mind?" She asked.

I raised a brow, staring straight ahead.

"You were painfully unhappy, VDM. And now, you're a completely different person."

I paused. "You're right. But I deserve to know the truth. Don't do this to me again."

I glanced toward her and she winced.

I hadn't meant to hurt her, and the response gave me pause. "I mean that as a friend. Just tell me the truth." I wasn't actually half as mad as I wanted to be. I could see where she was coming from, and I knew she meant well. I still trusted her more than I'd ever trust my own parents ever again.

She nodded, still looking contrite.

"I messed up. I know I did. I just thought that fate needed a little push," Kelly said.

"You're not fate," I said, already feeling exasperated.

"I feel like you deceived me," I admitted. I felt ashamed to be so vulnerable in the moment. The hardest part of being a secretly hopeful and optimistic person was people you trusted letting you down, and I'd had a lot of that in the past few days with my mother.

She reached across the center console and put an arm on my shoulder. "I truly am sorry for not telling you. I'm not sorry for what I did, but I'm sorry for not telling you about the files when I should have."

"I want to be madder at you, but I can't help thinking you came from a good place with it," I said, staring into the darkness ahead of us.

She cleared her throat, and I thought I heard the slightest of sniffles.

"Just… don't do it again, okay? As a friend. Or an assistant. But mostly a friend."

I glanced toward her and she nodded.

I PULLED up beside Julia's car — which, of course, there was absolutely no way I was letting her give back or pay for herself, despite the barrage of questions she'd asked me about it. I could treat my girlfriend to nice things without her having to feel guilty. Why else have money if not to shower it on the people you love?

"Remington, the car," Kelly scolded as I hopped out without even turning it off. I glanced back to see her lean over and press the ignition button, then follow me inside.

I was going to find out what was in the contract and I was going to give Alison a piece of my mind. I'd been so civil in the divorce. I'd agreed to almost everything she'd requested, including our house in Chicago and our Hilton Head vacation house. I'd agreed to a lump sum payment versus alimony. Her parents were wealthier than mine, she'd certainly pull through somehow. And this was how she was repaying my kindness? Just showing up at my house out of nowhere to cause trouble with the only woman I've ever loved? This was low, even for Alison.

I walked in the door, ready for a brawl. In a fight I imagined Julia could absolutely take Alison in terms of strength, but Alison was the type of woman who could stab another in the eye with a high heel and not even flinch. She was brutally resourceful and evil when she needed to be.

What I actually found inside my house surprised me: Five women sitting around in the great room, sipping drinks out of margarita glasses, laughing. Music was playing from the record player — Dolly Parton? A universally good choice, to be sure, but still a shock.

Alison was telling a story, tears streaming down her cheeks as the others burst into hysterical fits and giggles.

Kelly stood beside me, looking just as stunned as I felt.

Julia glanced up to see us standing there and startled, glancing at the large clock near the kitchen. "Oh, hey baby," she said, standing up as she walked over to me. She was flushed and smiling.

"Is everything okay?" I asked, my voice low. Had Alison drugged them? Brainwashed them?

She nodded. "Yeah, Ali was just telling us about the first time you tried to play polo."

Ali?

Alison stood, straightening the knee-length body contoured dress she was wearing. "Hi, Remington."

I looked around at the faces in the room, stunned into silence, and looked back down to Julia. "Can we talk for a moment in private?"

She nodded, pulling me out of the room and into a guest bedroom I usually forgot about. It was pitifully bare in there — clearly I never expected having guests.

"I broke approximately ninety-four traffic laws to get here and save you," I said, clenching my teeth. "I thought you were in trouble."

"I tried calling," she said, her brow furrowing. "To tell you not to worry."

I hadn't been looking at my phone, obviously.

"Why are you acting like pals with my ex-wife out there?" I asked, crossing my arms over my chest.

"First, I can be friends with whomever I would like. Second, I don't think she's here for a bad reason." She nodded definitively, as though that further proved her point.

"Then, *why* is she here?" I asked.

Julia shrugged, looking confused. "She wanted to talk to you."

"I have a phone."

"I think this was an in-person conversation."

I took a deep, cleansing, calming breath, trying to remember how much of the chamomile tea I'd actually had. Was that really just a few hours before? Had I only met the Board of Guardian just that day?

"What does she want to talk to me about?" I asked.

Julia shook her head. "She didn't say."

"Oh, that didn't come up?" I asked, raising my brows.

Julia narrowed her eyes at me. "I know you had a long day, and I know this isn't what you were expecting, but we're on the same team here, so get over yourself."

I blinked, sighing. "I don't want to fight with you," I said, wrapping my arms around her waist.

"I know you don't." She put her hands on my chest, running over my shoulders and down my arms. "So, I'm going to forgive your little brat attack there, but I need you to go out there and talk to her, or even wait until the morning, I don't care, but you have to sort this out once and for all."

"Brat attack?" I asked, furrowing my brow as I stared down at her.

"Oh yeah, when you are surprised, you instantly turn into a brat."

"I'm a grown ass woman. I am *not* a brat. It's just been a long day, and I have a lot to tell you." What I really wanted was to climb into my bathtub, pull Julia in, and try to piece out why my mother had broken us up and how Kelly had gone behind my back. I felt betrayed by both, but in different ways. It was hard to process and I just wanted to push away the rest of the world while still keeping Julia close.

She pushed onto her tiptoes to kiss my nose, then pulled out of my arms. "Do you want to talk to her alone or do you want me to be with you?"

I took her hand in mine, squeezing. "With me. Please."

I WATCHED Flossie pour Kelly a margarita and Quinn, the architect I'd just met who introduced herself with extreme professionalism, was cutting up a lime. What a strange new world I'd come home to. And yet, not the strangest thing that had happened to me in my own kitchen in the past week.

Alison and Julia had already disappeared to the upstairs loft where I said I'd join them in a moment.

Kelly pulled the file folder out of her bag and handed it to me, but she didn't let go of her end of it. "You okay?"

I nodded.

"Okay, it's kinda spicy," Flossie said with a shimmy, sliding a glass across the kitchen island toward Kelly. "Remington, you joining us in Margaritaville?"

I shook my head. I wanted to be clear-headed to talk to Alison.

"*Wasting away again in Margaritaville*," Cameron and Quinn launched into song almost immediately.

Well, that was my cue to leave.

I walked upstairs, down the hallway to find the secluded loft. It wasn't a big room, but it was cozy. And Julia had already planned exactly what furniture would suit the space so that we could drink hot cocoa and sit by the fireplace. It felt strange to have Alison here. I could sense that Julia thought so, as well. The mood was tense as I walked into the room.

"Why are you here?" I asked, sitting down on the sofa next to Julia. Alison sat in one of the overstuffed leather chairs that had been crammed into the space.

Julia squeezed my knee. "I think what Remi means is that your arrival feels a little sudden. Is everything okay?"

Not at all what I meant, but I was still grateful to Julia for smoothing down my rougher edges.

"I came as soon as your mother called," Alison said, tilting her head. "She told me that you were considering getting back together."

My mouth went dry with shock.

"Wh-what?" Julia asked, blinking in surprise.

Alison rolled her eyes. "Obviously I didn't believe it, but then she... well, it's kind of a long story." She waved her hand in the air dismissively.

I set the file down on the table, putting an arm around Julia's shoulders on the back of the couch. She was my rock, and I felt braver having her there.

"I don't want to be a pawn in our parents' game anymore." Alison lifted her chin in a show of confidence. "And I had to come here to make sure that we're united on that front."

Julia tensed beside me, then looked from Alison back to me.

"I just want a little context about the contract," I said, gesturing toward the file.

Alison leaned forward, opening up the file. She flipped through the photos with interest, then the text and phone logs. She scanned Curtis' contact, but paused at her own. Her brow furrowed.

"What is this?" She asked.

"If anyone should know, isn't it you?" I was done with the games.

She lifted up the piece of paper, looking from the front to the back. "That's my signature, but I never *signed* this. That's ridiculous." She held the paper close to her face, squinting at it. "This is all copied and pasted, anyway."

"Okay, can someone explain this to me?" Julia said, leaning forward. "What does the contract say?"

Alison took a deep, slow breath in. "I did sign something right when I first came to your parents' house in Virginia over Spring Break. It was just an NDA. I kind of thought it was overboard, but it wasn't this."

"You didn't think signing an NDA was weird?" Julia asked.

"Rich people are weird," Alison said casually. "I thought it was because they weren't comfortable with you being outed yet."

I narrowed my eyes.

"Then, what's on the piece of paper in your hand?" Julia asked.

Alison flipped the paper over again. "It basically states that I was agreeing to enter into a business relationship with the Van der Meer family, and that I was agreeing to a few stipulations. And then it has the NDA at the bottom. But I swear, Remington, I never signed this exact contract."

Julia looked even more confused.

I did my best to fill her in quickly — the contracts, the checks, my mother. Julia's eyes grew wider and wider.

"So, this is all about your parents controlling you?" She asked, looking between me and Alison.

"Yeah," the two of us said in stereo.

Julia fidgeted with a curl near her face, looking nervous and overwhelmed.

"The second I came out as bisexual, my parents said

that you and I would be perfect together. I think they probably put the idea in your parents' head," Alison said,
leaning back in her chair.

"And then I started talking about Julia and I moving to
Boston, and my mother probably figured you'd be a more
appropriate match."

"Well, I'm assuming your mother also knew I'd be
easier to control," Alison said, shaking her head. "Given
that my own parents had always called the shots and I'd
played along with it perfectly." She smiled, looking tired
and bitter. "To be honest, what I had with your father was
the first rebellious thing I'd ever done in my life."

I tensed, unsure what to say.

Julia, to my surprise, laughed. "That's awful," she said.

Alison grinned. "I know, right?" She shook her head. "I
didn't do that to hurt you, Remington. I did that to..." She
paused, as though looking for the right words. When she
found them, her voice was almost a whisper. "Feel
anything."

I almost felt bad for her. I had the freedom of escaping
into my career, climbing the corporate ladder by working
long days, sleeping at the office, staying on the hamster
wheel. Alison was on charity Boards and did god-knows-
what-else. I barely ever feigned interest.

We'd lived separately for years, making excuses about
how it was so much easier for her to be in Hilton Head
while I was in Chicago, or her in Virginia at her parents'
house while I was in South Carolina. We were like similar
magnetic forces in our unhappiness, unable to ever come
together.

I was miserable, and I should have realized she
was, too.

"I wanted to come here today to once and for all make
an alliance with you about our parents. No more being

under their control. From now on, I choose my own happiness." She straightened her posture.

Julia sniffled, and I looked over to see that she was wiping at her eyes. "I'm sorry, that's just really inspiring."

Alison's determined expression softened. "You two were meant to be together, and I'm so happy that you are. I promise I never knew about your breakup, and I didn't have a part in it."

I didn't know if I believed her, but I couldn't decide what harm taking her at her word would do now.

"And I think I'm going to cut my parents out of my life," Alison added, swallowing. "So, if they contact you, you don't know how to reach me. Understand?"

I nodded. "I'm thinking I might have to do something similar."

This conversation was the most we'd talked in years. Even through the divorce, I'd agreed quickly just to get it over with. I should have known by how fast she'd agreed to everything, too, that she wanted out of the marriage just as much as I did.

Alison stood, taking a deep breath as though she was trying to be brave during something scary. I felt the same. "One more favor?"

I looked up at her.

She smoothed down her dress. "Can I stay the night here? I think I've had a few too many of Flossie's margaritas to get back to the airport safely."

I was about to tell her I'd find her a hotel in town, but Julia interrupted me. "Of course," she said smiling warmly.

CHAPTER NINETEEN

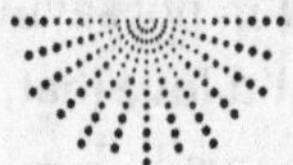

JULIA

I REACHED TO TURN OFF THE LIGHT AS SOON AS ALISON LEFT the room. Bathed in darkness, we could see clearly outside, with the view extending across the valley, over the peaks, and to the sky.

Remi sighed, rubbing at her face. "I feel like I've been run over by a semi."

"Baby, you've gone through a lot today," I said, pulling her into me to rest her head on my chest.

She wrapped her arms around me, curling her body into mine, letting me hold her. "My mother, Alison, Kelly... everyone lies."

I pet her hair, letting my fingers brush her scalp and slide through the soft, light strands. "Not everyone."

She squeezed me in her arms. "Not everyone. Not the ones who really matter."

We sat in silence for a moment.

"I'm going to call my therapist in the morning," she said quietly, nuzzling me.

"I think that's a really good idea." I kissed her forehead, staring out the window. Dark, vast, and yet, calming in the unknowns.

She took a deep breath, tensing beside me. "And I don't want to upset you, but maybe we should think about couples therapy. I don't even know what a healthy, loving relationship looks like. I'm not saying—"

"Baby, I know. And I'd love that." I stopped her, trying to tell her firmly that I agreed.

"Really?" She kissed my collarbone.

"Really." I'd do anything to make sure we could be happy together forever.

I heard footsteps behind us and turned to find Stormy sauntering into the loft, looking excited that she'd found us. She put her paws on the sofa next to me, wagging her tail as she stared up at us. She slurped Remi's cheek, then hopped up to the spot that I patted, curling into the other side of me.

"I feel like we're on the edge of big change, you know?" Remi said, reaching out a hand to scratch Stormy under her wrinkly chin.

I agreed with a small hum, sighing.

"I don't know what the future holds. I don't know what my career looks like. I don't know how relationships should actually work, you know?" Remi continued.

I took a deep breath, trying not to interrupt the point she was obviously struggling to make.

She pushed herself up to look at me, her forehead wrinkled in concern. I could barely make out the expression around her blue eyes in the darkness, but I could tell that she was worried I already had one foot out the door.

My chest squeezed at her tone. I moved my hand to cup her face, my thumb brushing the soft skin of her cheek. "You know what I always wondered about?"

"Hmm?" She stared up at me.

I paused, trying to find the right explanation for my thoughts. "You know how Neruda says, '*A swan, a tree, something far away and happy*' as stories he tells his sad lover to make her feel better?"

"You want to discuss poetry right now?" Even in the dim light, I could tell that her expression had changed to one of amusement.

"Just hear me out." Maybe I was going about this the wrong way. "He says two literal objects, then that vague line about happiness being something far away. I never really got it before now."

She stared up at me in silence as Stormy shifted beside me, sighing and getting comfortable. Loud laughter came from another part of the house.

"Someday, this will feel easier. We'll find a routine. We'll settle into a comfortable life together. We'll have a better foundation for the storms. Until then, we just have to focus on what's in front of us. We have each other, and the dog, and this house, and a massive renovation project, and maybe a new job. Forever seems overwhelming, and it feels so far away. Let's focus on the small happiness, the small comforts and beauties that are happening right now."

"*Oh to be able to celebrate you with all the words of joy,*" she murmured, settling back to rest her head on my chest. "That's the best line of the poem, of any poem."

I kissed the top of her head. "I much prefer when you celebrate me without any words at all," I teased.

She lifted her head again, grinning. "That can be arranged."

"Maybe after we get these partiers safely to their beds?" I said.

She groaned. "If you insist."

• • •

THE NEXT MORNING, I stood in the kitchen pouring myself a cup of coffee as Cameron walked into the room behind me, wrapping her arms around my waist and laying her head on my back. "Why did you let me drink all of the ingredients for a headache?" She groaned.

"Altitude is a bitch," I joked, reaching for a water glass as she remained a koala on my back. I handed it back to her.

She stood, taking a seat on a barstool as she sipped at the water. I opened a cupboard and handed her a bottle of Advil.

Flossie walked into the kitchen looking bright-eyed and bushy-tailed. Quinn dragged behind her, silver bedhead sticking in all directions. Cameron silently passed her the bottle of Advil.

"Remington isn't going to fire me for getting drunk, right?" Quinn asked in a hushed whisper, apologizing as she stole a drink of Cameron's water to take the Advil with.

"She doesn't have the power to fire you. I'm the General Contractor. I call the shots." I grinned into my coffee cup.

"I most definitely am still the boss," Remi said, walking into the kitchen, but she was grinning with a mischievous twinkle in her eye. She poured a cup of coffee and nuzzled my neck. She was certainly in a good mood after talking to her therapist for the past hour.

We'd talked long into the night about what she wanted to bring up to her therapist first, and she'd surprised me by what she wanted to focus on first: grudges and forgiveness, specifically when it came to Kelly. I'd been Team Kelly all the way, but Remi had a hard time letting go of the principle of the matter. I'd pointed out that she'd dropped the grudge against me rather easily.

"That's different. You're you. And I love you."

Remembering that phrase now, I turned and kissed her. Softly, assuringly.

Flossie groaned. "Get a room." Cameron raised her water glass in a silent, "hear, hear" gesture. I slid a cup of coffee across the kitchen island for her.

Alison appeared, looking awkward. "Quinn, did you need a ride back to Denver this morning? I can take you."

Quinn nodded, holding her forehead. "Maybe after the pills kick in."

Flossie reached out, taking Quinn's hand. "I think that was my motto in the 60s."

I nearly choked on my coffee.

"Gives me just enough time to show you my house." Flossie beamed.

"Hope you like clutter," Remi muttered, but she was grinning. She winked at Flossie.

"By clutter, do you mean anything that signals a real, live human being might live there? I know that's definitely something you don't know anything about," Flossie said, gesturing to the great room. "Thank god Julia came back into your life."

"Agreed," Remi said with a smile.

Kelly stepped into the kitchen, looking perfectly pressed and presentable. "Did I hear there would be a ride back to Denver? Can I get in on that? This elevation is really messing with my sinuses. Do you think it might snow soon?" She pressed on her cheeks under her eyes.

Flossie shrugged. "Weirder things have happened."

"Can I talk to you before you leave?" Remi asked, turning to Kelly.

Kelly nodded, her expression completely blank. If she

was nervous, she didn't show it. I wondered idly if she could give me lessons on that kind of control.

Remi poured her a cup of coffee and handed it to her before leading the way out of the room. We'd talked about it last night, and I hope her therapist had given her solid advice for talking to Kelly about trust and the future. She loved Kelly, and I thought Kelly had obviously done something right and shouldn't be punished, per se, given that she'd gotten us back together.

Flossie and Quinn disappeared, and Cameron and Alison chatted as I poured a bowl of cereal.

Alison asked if we had any fresh fruit — the answer was limes, but apparently limes didn't go in a fresh parfait. She settled for a bowl of cereal with me.

The night before, when she'd showed up out of the blue, I was ready to punch her in the face. After the initial awkwardness, she'd been the first to apologize, to quickly explain why she was there. Once I heard her out and heard that Remi's mother had contacted her, I was a little more willing to listen. She simply wanted to make sure she and Remi were on the same page for future assaults. Because, she explained, Remi's parents would be relentless.

Cameron had actually been the one to completely break the ice by asking her about her outfit. They'd begun bonding over a mutual brand campaign they'd done sponsored posts for on Instagram, and then it was over.

Alison had won over Flossie by hooking up her own phone to the record player speaker AUX cord and playing Loretta Lynn.

Once Cameron and Flossie were on board, it was hard not to follow suit. We'd started talking, and I had been able to set aside my ego once I had the stunning realization that even if Alison were there to try to win back Remi, I was confident that Remi wouldn't have it. What we had was special, and Alison was gorgeous, sure, but there was no spark to her stories when she talked about Rem.

After all these years, I thought I'd hate her more, but she was actually very funny and kind, as far as I could tell.

Remington Van der Meer was my person, and I trusted her. Even in her absence, I was secure in what we had. In that moment more than ever.

CAMERON MADE A GAGGING noise and scooted away from the cereal — apparently the smell of the multigrain squares were really getting to her.

Alison reached over and rubbed her back. "I'm sorry, Cammie. You want me to make you some lemon water?"

"Absolutely not," Cameron grumbled, laying her head on the countertop.

Remi and Kelly returned after about twenty minutes, but she was still talking as she walked back into the room. "A locked gate, really?"

"Yeah, with an access code," Kelly said, looking down at her phone.

Remi raised her eyebrows as she considered it. "Seems like overkill."

"And you really don't think they'll pull an Alison and just show up?" Kelly asked.

"I'm *right* here," Alison said with a mouthful of cereal.

"I'm just saying, if you're going to cut them completely out, let's do it right." Kelly said. "And if you don't want to get a restraining order, you're going to need other safeguards."

"They won't show up here," Alison said with confidence.

"How are you so certain?" I asked.

"When we announced we were getting a divorce, they never showed up at our home. Any of our homes. They always summoned us to theirs. I think they like having the home field advantage," Alison explained.

"That is a good point," Remi said, nodding. "They find it far too uncomfortable to meet you halfway. It's always on their own terms."

"Exactly." Alison pointed her spoon toward Remi. "So, I don't think you have anything to worry about."

Kelly gave her a polite, forced smile. "Thank you for your insight, Miss Dawes."

Remi nodded. "Okay, let's table this for now, and I'll talk to Julia about what will make her the most comfortable."

I nodded but took a deep breath, feeling overwhelmed by the idea. I saw that Stormy was standing at the patio door asking to go outside. I excused myself, relieved to have a reason to step outside and bask in the quietness for a moment. Maybe Remi was onto something with the hermit tendencies.

I walked down the stairs with Stormy, taking in the crisp, morning air. It was so quiet, so still. I longed for the silent refuge it had been just days before, when the biggest problem I had to worry about was my inability to keep my hands off of Remi.

And yet, I was grateful for the curveball that life had thrown at me. I was grateful to have Remi back in my life. Like we were always meant to be. A second chance at happiness. We had so much time to make up. Ten years. How could we ever get them back?

"A swan, a tree," Remi murmured behind me.

I turned, looking up at her. I was afraid to disturb the stillness of the perfect morning. But it wasn't truly still, was it? The birds were trilling, the crickets were awake, and the forest stretching out for miles before us was alive and well. "I love you," I said, reaching for her.

"And I love you," she whispered back, taking the last step towards me.

EPILOGUE

One Year later
Julia

"Jude, everyone's going to be here soon," Remi called up the stairs.

"I'll be right there," I called, leaning over the bed to readjust the picture frame one last time. It had been the bane of my existence for the past week. Just slightly crooked whenever I looked at it, like it waited for me to walk away before sagging a bit to the left.

I took a step back, looking up at the wall. Our bedroom had turned out exactly how I'd been dreaming. The main bedroom and the bathroom were where Remi let me fully splurge without any of her own opinion, so of course, it was lush, featuring deep colors and plush fabrics throughout.

I especially loved the patterned floor tile in the bathroom, as well as an updated version of the world's largest tub.

But in the entire house, this one wall above our bed was my favorite. I'd made it an accent wall by wallpapering it with a special pattern I'd gotten from Flossie after seeing it in her house.

The wallpaper was navy blue with white and grey swans patterned asymmetrically throughout. It had a slight metallic sheen to it that made it feel extra special. I'd only done half of the wall in the swans, accenting the bottom half with a deep gray wainscotting.

I heard Remi's shoes click on the hardwood behind me and felt her arms wrap around my waist. She laid her chin on my shoulder, looking at the wall.

"It's perfect. Everything's perfect. And ready. And everyone will be here soon, so stop staring at it," she said.

"I can't help it. It's my favorite part of the entire house."

"The bed?" She laughed, holding my hair back and warming my neck with her breath, sending goosebumps all over my body.

"I mean, the bed *is* perfection," I admitted, reaching out to touch the post near us. I'd gone with my gut, staining it a light oak to brighten up the rest of the otherwise heavy colors and textures in the room. Even Remi had admitted that it'd turned out perfectly. "But I like this one wall."

"The entire house? You designed, oversaw, fired a plumber, redid the floors twice, and decorated the entire house, and this is your favorite part?" She laughed at me, kissing my cheek.

I nodded, looking at the picture of us. We were standing in the forest, I was in a fancy dress and she was in a fancy suit. It was taken from a distance, so that upon looking at the image, you might not even find us at the very bottom. A photographer had taken it on a special day not too long ago, and I'd immediately gotten it blown up, knowing exactly where it'd go.

"Swans," Remi said, pointing to the wallpaper.

"Trees," I said, smiling at the image, waiting for her to point out the obvious.

"Something incredibly close and incredibly happy," she said before I could say the real phrase, spinning me in her arms.

She kissed me, holding me close, her lips were warm and pliable. Her kiss felt familiar, but still stirred warmth in my entire body. I was once floating from her kisses, but now they grounded me, reminding me that no matter what, we had each other.

I smiled up at her once we broke the kiss, feeling firm and solid in my happiness.

"Now, I do just have to say that you have Stormy hair all over your blazer, baby," she said, digging in her nightstand for the lint remover. She made me turn again and rolled the back.

"Be careful," I said, smoothing down the front of the buttery soft velvet. It was the nicest article of clothing I owned, bought with my own money after securing the design of a new hotel renovation downtown. Flossie had introduced me to her friend, who owned the building, and showed him some of my work, and voilà. I'd been quite busy with the house renovations, but Remi had encouraged me to take breaks to keep pursuing my other dreams. She'd even flown me to Santa Fe to work on a project with Quinn just last week.

"Yeah, yeah, I know, it's the lucky blazer," Remi said from behind me, but I could hear the smile in her voice.

She helped me de-fur and we walked downstairs hand-in-hand. The place looked similar, but now with life. Remi would have happily lived in a brutal minimalist home for the rest of her life, but together we'd found a common ground between my maximalism and her discerning eye.

We'd had a few compromises and together, we created a place where we both felt completely comfortable. It was like the day I set foot in this mansion, Remi had made it clear that it was my home, too. She'd asked me to move in almost a week after our second-first kiss.

The doorbell rang and I walked through the foyer to open the front door. Cameron and her boyfriend, Markus, stood on the step. Her eyes were wide. "Seriously with the lack of guard rails around here."

"I know, right? Go sit down and drink some water," I commanded.

She laughed, hugging me.

Someone I didn't recognize walked onto the porch, looking uncertain of himself.

"Jonah," Remi said excitedly, and I made Cameron step inside so that Remi could hug her friend.

"There are worse caves to be a hermit in, Rem," Jonah said, smiling. Remi introduced us, and I shook his hand, inviting him in. I'd heard so many stories of their adventures together, and I was looking forward to getting to know him. He was staying for a few days with a rock climbing trip after the housewarming party.

Overhearing something Remi said to Jonah, Cameron's boyfriend struck up a conversation with him about the area, and I barely had a moment to shoot Cameron a thankful thumbs up before Flossie walked up to the patio.

She called behind her. "You coming today or would you rather party alone outside?"

Quinn appeared from the side of the house, holding up her phone. "Sorry, I was just taking pictures. I had an idea about the garage." She winked at me, taking Flossie's hand as we welcomed them inside.

Flossie rolled her eyes. "I've seen it a billion times, but I can't resist a free tequila bar."

"Ah, so my personalized invitation had worked," I said, giving her a high five.

My parents pulled into the driveway and I ran outside to meet them, throwing my arms around my mom the instant she stepped out the door. I briefly saw that Remi was hugging my father, telling him how happy she was that they'd been able to make in. The past year, my parents had taken on the role of welcoming Remi with open arms into our family. She didn't talk to her own parents anymore, and I knew that took a toll on her that she wasn't ready to admit even to herself, but my parents had stepped up to help fill the gap however they could.

Seeing Remi look at my father with admiration melted my entire heart.

My parents had come to the house for Christmas, but we'd been tearing up the kitchen at the time, so we'd grilled on the back deck, Remi and my father standing outside in snow to flip steaks.

"And there's my granddaughter," Mom said excitedly, looking past me.

I turned to see Stormy standing on the porch, wiggling excitedly. We'd promised Stormy's first owner that we'd work with a trainer to make sure she would never run away, and the porch had become Stormy's hard limit. She wouldn't even walk with me down to the mailbox unless I put a leash on her, giving her permission. Her freshly bathed brown fur glittered in the sunlight and her tongue lolled out of her mouth as she smiled and danced, waiting for my mom to greet her properly.

"You're more excited about Stormy than my new kitchen?" I asked, surprised.

Mom looked at me like I'd just asked her if the sky was blue. "Of course," she said, pushing past me.

I laughed, watching her walk inside.

I turned to follow her, getting distracted as Remi yelled out a hello to someone coming up the drive. Kelly leaned out her car window, waving. Remi greeted her like an old friend, hugging her and ushering her and her husband inside.

I looked up at the house before me. It looked the same from the outside — sprawling, towering, large, but not as offensive as I'd once thought it. Inside, it was entirely new, reflecting the two of us. Remi's minimalist sectional sofa, my vibrantly painted kitchen cabinets, Remi's dark hard-wood floors, my plush Turkish rugs scattered throughout. It was warm, it was classic, it was fun, and it was us.

Remi reached for me, taking my hand in hers. She interlocked our fingers, pulling me towards her.

"You ready to tell them?" She asked, her eyebrows raised.

I took a deep breath, nodding as butterflies swirled in my stomach.

She squeezed my hand. "They'll be happy for us."

"Even though we didn't tell anyone, and it's been three weeks?" I grimaced exaggeratedly, but leaned in to kiss her shoulder.

"Have we really been newlyweds for three whole weeks?" Remi asked, kissing the back of my hand. We'd eloped without witnesses — self-solemnizing our commit-ment with just a photographer present. And, now, we were about to tell all of the people we loved the most under the guise of a housewarming party.

I smoothed down my lucky blazer one last time, tucking a wayward curl behind my ear. "Okay, I'm ready."

THANK YOU!

Thank you so much for reading Something Far Away and Happy! Your support means everything to my little indie heart.

Want to join my not-spammy newsletter and get sneak peeks of all my new books? You can sign up at:

bryceoakley.com/subscribe

ACKNOWLEDGMENTS

A big thank you to my wife, whom I still love even when she won't let me renovate our entire house, or even buy new seasonal throw pillows at Target. I get it, you're rational, "we have enough," whatever, babe. You're my something close and happy, always.

Couldn't have written this without the constant enthusiasm and help from my sister, the one true Flossie stan.

DJs, you continue to inspire me to keep writing. Love our little community.

S, thank you for being the best part of the internet. Thank you for always finding my dumb typos and talking through the good and the bad.

Maxx Steele, pleeeeeeease please write your book?

Of course, most importantly, thank you so SO much to all of my readers. I read every email, every tweet, every DM, and I cherish your insights and reactions.

P.S. — I took some artistic liberties with this book, so don't worry, I know there's no airport in Breckenridge and I know there's currently a global pandemic, but not in this book. Be the change you wish to see and all that.

ABOUT THE AUTHOR

Bryce grew up in the mountains of Colorado with a taste for adventure and a head full of clouds. She never grew out of either.

She lives in Denver with her wife, two extremely cute and spoiled rescue dogs who most definitely inspire every dog character, and a feisty little cat who thinks it's dinnertime *all the time.*